Diablo – Freed From Fear

Gabi Adam

Diablo –
Freed From Fear

Copyright: © Gabi Adam 2005
The plot and the names of the characters are entirely fictional.
Original Title: Fesseln der Angst
Cover photo: © Bob Langrish
Cover layout: Stabenfeldt A/S
Translated by Barclay House Publishing
Typeset by Roberta L. Melzl
Editor: Bobbie Chase
Printed in Germany, 2007

ISBN: 1-933343-57-5

Stabenfeldt, Inc.
457 North Main Street
Danbury, CT 06811
www.pony.us

For my horse-fanatic kids Jessy, Andy, and Jenny

Chapter 1

It had been several weeks since Cathy Sutherland's serious riding accident on her horse, Rashid – an accident that fractured her pelvis. Cathy's friends, Lillian Bates, Kevin Thomas, and Ricki Sulai, would never forget that day, because it was Ricki's fourteenth birthday.

After the terrible experience, Cathy decided never to ride again, and never again to go near Rashid. Even the thought of the horse caused her to panic.

"Never in a zillion years would I have guessed something like this could happen," said Ricki dejectedly to Lillian and Kevin, as the three of them readied their horses, Diablo, Doc Holliday, and Sharazan, in the Sulais' stable for their afternoon ride.

Rashid, who was owned by Carlotta Mancini, a former circus performer, looked over the top of his stall excitedly at his four-legged stable companions. He seemed expectant, as if wondering whether he would be allowed to go out onto the meadows with them.

"The poor thing! I really feel sorry for him! Do you

think we should take him with us on a lead?" Kevin asked, buckling the snaffle onto his roan. "The boy just doesn't understand what's going on. Cathy used to ride him every day, and it's just not the same with us taking turns riding him so he gets some exercise."

"Do you know that Carlotta is thinking of looking for another rider for him? She's begun to give up any hope that Cathy will change her mind," reported Lillian.

Ricki frowned. "That means that here, in our stable, a stranger we know nothing about could be coming and going soon. I really hate to think about it," she grumbled.

"I don't like it either, but we should think about Rashid," interrupted Kevin, and he stroked the dun horse affectionately across his muzzle.

"I know." Ricki nodded, although she was not the least bit happy about it. For the good of the horse, the friends would have to "bite the bullet," so to speak, and accept a new rider for Rashid.

Suddenly, however, her face lit up. "You know what, we're being stupid!" she exploded.

"Oh?" Lillian grinned. "So what else is new?"

"That's so brutal, when someone we know and love says something like that to us," replied Kevin, pretending to be hurt, and Ricki laughed out loud.

"Seriously, though, why don't we help Carlotta find a new rider? We know enough kids from the riding club who would probably love to ride Rashid. What do you two think?" Ricki looked expectantly at her friends.

Lillian and Kevin eyed each other.

"Well, basically I think your idea is great, Ricki, but

when I think about it, and go over the people we know, I don't think there's anyone who would fit in here." Lillian shrugged her shoulders.

"Hmm, Sasha might be the best bet, or Justin, he's cool." Kevin wrinkled his forehead, deep in thought.

"Sasha? Never." Ricki shook her head firmly. "She is so arrogant! And Justin, yeah, he's okay, but he just rides because he thinks it's the cool thing to do!"

"Of course, Kevin would like to have another guy here at the stable. Up to now, we girls have been the majority, but Sasha is worth considering. She's a really good rider, and —" Lillian started.

"Well, if I have to see that snob here every day, I'll move out!" Ricki interrupted her friend.

"Ricki, have you forgotten that this is your family's stable? You can't just move out with Diablo," teased Kevin.

"I don't care. If Sasha comes, I'll move to Carlotta's ranch with Diablo!"

"You would really board Diablo at Carlotta's ranch? That's crazy!"

"No, it isn't. Hey, people, do you notice something? It's already starting. Just the idea of somebody invading our group is making us crazy," responded Ricki.

"And who was the one who just had a crazy idea? That was you, dearest Ricki, when you —"

"Okay, then, I won't move out, but it doesn't have to be Sasha, does it? There's got to be somebody who would fit in with us, and would be a good rider for Rashid."

Kevin and Lillian nodded in agreement.

"We'll just have to take our time looking. A few days

more or less won't make any difference. Now, let's go riding."
Kevin said, leading Sharazan toward the stable door. "Should
we take Rashid with us or not?"

"Who's going to hold his reins?" asked Lillian.

"I'll take him. He runs best beside Sharazan," replied
Kevin. He tied Sharazan to a post in the stable corridor,
opened Rashid's stall and led the dun out. As he fastened
the snaffle it was obvious how happy the animal was that he
didn't have to stay behind in the stable.

Chico, the little donkey, and Salina, the pony mare,
looked over their stall walls at the goings-on.

"You two can go out onto the paddock afterward," Lillian
promised the two little animals. "Harry and Jake will be here
soon to take you."

She had hardly finished her sentence when Ricki's younger
brother and the elderly stable hand appeared on the scene.

"Oh, boy, you're taking Rashid with you again. Can I sit
on him?" asked Harry, although he already knew that Ricki
would turn him down.

"No way, Harry. How many times do I have to explain it to
you? You don't ride well enough yet to come with us on our
ride. And I think, after what happened to Cathy, neither Carlotta
nor Mom would be very happy if I let you ride with us."

Harry pouted.

"Don't be upset, they don't want me with them either,"
Jake winked at him. "We guys are going to brush Chico and
Salina until they shine and these riders turn green with envy,
and then we're going to take them down to the paddock.
Afterward you can come to my house, and we can watch a
western together, if you like."

8

"Cool!" Harry clapped his hands delightedly. Watching TV at Jake's always meant that there would be a huge bowlful of popcorn.

Grateful, Ricki nodded to the old man. The three friends led their horses out of the stable and tightened the girths, and then they mounted and trotted off at an easy pace.

"You have to stay home, unfortunately," Ricki said, glancing affectionately at Rosie and her three puppies who came running up, their tails wagging, wanting to go with them. "Don't be sad. When we get back we'll take a walk together, okay?" she said gently. As if the dog had understood every word, Rosie let out a bark and chased her puppies away.

Smiling, Ricki watched the animals disappear behind the house. She was so happy that Rosie had found a real home with the Sulais. Ricki had found the abandoned pregnant dog on her fourteenth birthday, while she had been out riding.

"Can we get going, please, before Rashid turns around a few more times and twists his reins out of my hand?" asked Kevin, grinning.

"Sure!"

"What are we waiting for? We'll never get better weather than today's," laughed Lillian happily as she picked up her reins.

*

Cathy lay on her bed, leafing through a fashion magazine. "Who's going to wear this?" she asked herself quietly. The super-thin model was wearing a dress made of strips of white fabric. She looked as if someone had wrapped her

9

in endless rolls of toilet paper. To top it off, her long dark hair was teased into an impossible hairstyle and a crooked knitting needle was stuck through the mass of hair.

"That's really gross! Why didn't they just weave in two toilet bowl brushes while they were at it?" In a bad mood, Cathy shut the magazine and tossed it onto the floor. Then she turned onto her back, frustrated, put her hands behind her head and looked toward the window.

The sun was shining and a wonderful bright blue sky invited her to go outside and enjoy nature on the gorgeous fall day.

"Swimming is always good exercise," the doctor who was handling her postoperative care had said. But Cathy just didn't feel like going swimming again. It was too late in the season to go swimming in Echo Lake, and she couldn't stand to have her mother drive her to the Y yet again.

It's getting so that I can't bear to see any more water! she thought. *No one, not even Ricki, is going to get me to go swimming again!*

Horses. Suddenly, Cathy realized that her friends wouldn't be calling her today. Days like this belonged to their animals, and she was sure that Ricki, Lillian, and Kevin were already on their afternoon ride through the meadows. They wouldn't call her until they finished exercising their horses. She felt really sorry for herself at the thought of being excluded from their friendship and activities.

Come on, you're not being fair, her conscience scolded her. *You used to be just like them, didn't you? And you can't expect your friends to change their lives just because you don't want anything more to do with horses!*

But that's completely different! Cathy tried to justify her point of view. *The animals weren't more important to me than my friends!*

Are you sure?

"Yes!" She spoke the little word out loud just as the door opened.

"Cathy, I'm going shopping. Do you want to come with me?" Mrs. Sutherland looked curiously at her daughter, but Cathy just shook her head miserably.

"No! I don't feel like it."

"Okay, but don't complain to me later that you're bored," responded her mother.

Actually Cathy would have loved to stroll slowly through the town and shop with her mother, but the prospect of listening to a two-hour speech from her mother, as she often did, made her dread it. Mrs. Sutherland would tell her again how happy she was that Cathy wasn't going to get on horses anymore, and that she wouldn't be hanging out at that horrible Carlotta's house.

It seemed to Cathy that her mother wanted to increase her fear of horses rather than help her regain her sense of security.

Cathy got up slowly and turned on her little television. By coincidence the first thing that appeared on the screen was a jumping event. And just at that moment, a horse and his rider crashed into an oxer.

Cathy turned off the TV immediately, with trembling fingers. Shakily, she wiped her hand across her eyes.

"Is this ever going to stop?" she asked herself. "I'm so tired of this!" she screamed suddenly. "This isn't normal!

I don't want to be afraid anymore!" Cathy sat down on her rocking chair and hugged her stuffed panda. Miserable, she started to rock back and forth slowly.

The loud ring of Cathy's cell phone startled her.

"No!" she screamed at the phone. "I don't want to go swimming, I don't want to go have a sundae, and I certainly don't want to play video games at the arcade! Just leave me alone!" And as though the caller at the other end of the line had understood, the cell phone stopped ringing as abruptly as it had started.

*

For weeks, Carlotta had tried her best to convince Cathy's mother how important it was for the girl to overcome her fear caused by the accident. Otherwise, Carlotta warned, it was possible that Cathy would be afraid of horses for the rest of her life, and her love of life — as well as her confidence and self-esteem — would suffer.

"You don't really think that I would ever let my daughter get into a saddle again?" Cathy's mother fumed, fed up with the conversation. She would have liked to ask Carlotta to leave her home right then.

"But one has nothing at all to do with the other! No one is asking Cathy to ride again! It's about her overcoming her fear and realizing that the accident happened because of a chain of unlucky coincidences that had nothing to do with Rashid. Cathy's appendix burst. She fell! It's not as if Rashid was responsible, and yet he's being blamed, and turned into the focal point of her fear. Right now, it looks as if Cathy has given up on everything."

"I know how it looks!" Mrs. Sutherland interrupted Carlotta angrily. "And don't try to tell me what's good for my daughter! I'm glad that she won't even say the word 'horse'!"

Carlotta sighed deeply and went to the door, but she turned one last time toward Cathy's mother. "I think you need to realize that you're feeding Cathy's fear instead of helping her to conquer it," she said softly.

"That is the limit, Mrs. Mancini! Now get out! And don't you dare come back here again!" Cathy's mother threatened. Even as she spoke, she realized that her reaction had only confirmed what Carlotta had said, and that made Mrs. Sutherland even more furious than she already was.

She slammed the door behind Rashid's owner and hoped that her daughter hadn't heard any of their conversation.

*

As she did so often in the days since the accident, Carlotta reviewed the scene in her mind and finally realized that she couldn't do anything for Cathy as long as Cathy's mother remained stubborn. With the realization that she would never be able to win back Cathy for Rashid, Carlotta's hopes were dashed.

She sighed softly and walked slowly toward the telephone in her kitchen, but it took a few more seconds for Carlotta to bring herself to pick up the receiver and dial the number she had cut out of the newspaper.

"Courier advertising department, Mary Bolton speaking. How may I help you?" said the voice on the other end of the line.

"Carlotta Mancini here. I'd like to put a small ad in the

paper. Please write this down: 'Is anyone looking for a riding opportunity, at no cost, on a gentle gelding, near —'"

"Riding opportunity?" the receptionist interrupted, curious. "And at no cost?"

"Yes," confirmed Carlotta brusquely.

"Hey, I know someone like that! A girl, thirteen years old, and she's been riding for five years."

Carlotta was interested. "Hmm, she sounds promising. Could you give me her address? She should call me if she's interested."

The woman laughed. "My daughter will be delighted! Okay, Mrs. Mancini, I'll send her to you. Shall I put the ad in anyway?"

"I think I'll interview your daughter first; maybe I won't need to place the ad after all." Absentmindedly, Carlotta dropped the receiver back onto the hook.

"I'm sorry, Cathy," she said softly. "I've thought this over for a long time, but I have to think of Rashid, and the way it's looking now, you won't be able to see him even if you want to."

*

The friends had finally decided to go riding around Echo Lake.

"We haven't been here in ages," exclaimed Ricki when she saw the lake stretching out in front of her.

"True. Does anyone mind if we take a little break?" asked Kevin. "Rashid has been pretty frisky, and I think a break would do my arm good."

"Okay, then," Lillian jumped down enthusiastically from the saddle and stretched. She unbuckled Holli's bit, so that

14

her horse could graze a little on the strip of meadow along the edge of the lake.

Seconds later, Diablo, Sharazan, and Rashid were also nibbling on the fresh grass.

"You know, I'm having trouble talking to Cathy. I have to pay close attention to every word I say, to keep myself from mentioning horses," said Lillian. "After all, Mrs. Sutherland has forbidden us to bring up that topic when we're talking with her daughter. Actually, I think it's really stupid. How is Cathy going to come to terms with her fear if she's not allowed to face it? What do you two think?"

"I feel the same way. I keep catching myself, wanting to tell her something about a ride, the way I used to. Mrs. Sutherland's weird, if you ask me. I'm glad she's not *my* mother!" answered Ricki, vehemently.

"Well, you know your mother has her problems with horses, too. I think she 'dies a thousand deaths', as the saying goes, every time you and Diablo go out for a ride. But the way Mrs. Sutherland is acting just isn't normal!"

Kevin, who was crouching between Sharazan and Rashid on the ground, shook his head in bewilderment. "I agree. Cathy should start getting used to horses again, gradually, by herself. But only if she wants to, of course. If not, it wouldn't make any sense."

"That's exactly what I think."

"Me too!"

The friends looked at each other for a while, before Ricki said what had been going through her mind for quite some time. "Why don't we just do it, then?"

Lillian made a face. "If only it were that easy. Look, one

15

false word from us, and Mrs. Sutherland would probably forbid us from talking to her daughter forever! She's threatened us like that before, plenty of times!"

"And? Does that really scare you?" retorted Ricki. "I mean, after all, we see Cathy every day at school, and we talk. Mrs. Sutherland can't keep tabs on us there, can she?"

"Well, okay, but what if Cathy's condition gets worse because of our therapy experiment? I mean, that could happen, couldn't it?" Kevin regarded his girlfriend seriously.

"You can't win without taking risks. I think we should at least try," suggested Ricki.

"But in a way, it really is a risk, Ricki, you can't deny that. I'd like nothing more than to see Cathy the way she used to be, but I don't think we're the right people for this kind of 'shock treatment'. We have no idea what might happen."

"Lillian, you're the one who started this conversation! And anyway, who better to help Cathy than her best friends?" Ricki just didn't want to accept the fact that the change in her friend could be permanent.

"A psychologist would be more appropriate and better qualified than we are."

"So you really think that some shrink could make Cathy get over her horse phobia? You're not serious, are you? Who, if not us, knows how she was before the accident? How much she loved Rashid, how much she loved going riding, and how many happy hours she spent with us in the stable? What does a therapist know about that? And I'm sure her mother won't tell the therapist, since it might actually manage to *cure* Cathy of her phobia." Ricki was really getting worked up.

Instead of answering, Lillian and Kevin stared straight ahead. Yeah, Ricki was right, but . . .

"Do you think Cathy is happy like this?" Ricki went on. "Absolutely not! And you know what else? She may be waiting for someone to talk to her about the whole mess. And one more thing; I'm *going* to talk to her about this, even if Mama Sutherland chases me to the ends of the earth afterward!"

"Whoa! Ricki has spoken!" exclaimed Kevin, but no one laughed.

"Funny, Kevin! Really funny! You didn't understand anything I said!" Ricki was mad.

"Listen, Ricki, I know that I'm dense, but really, I understood everything. I just wonder whether you're doing Cathy a favor or not."

"What do you mean?"

"Well, after all, Carlotta has been trying, too, and she's had absolutely no success with Cathy or Mrs. Sutherland. And if Carlotta can't get through to her, how are you, or we, going to manage it?" asked Kevin in a gentle voice. Ricki couldn't speak for a few minutes.

"I don't know," the girl finally answered hesitantly. "All I know is that we have to help Cathy, somehow, that I'm sure of."

"Ricki, I know you have a really close relationship with Cathy," said Lillian, putting her hand on her shoulder. "After all, she was your best friend even before you and I got to know each other. You know her much better than all of us put together; still, you can't do anything. *We* can't do anything without thinking about it first, without considering

17

the possible consequences. If we did more damage than good to Cathy, that would be awful, wouldn't it?"

Ricki thought it over for a minute and then nodded. "I guess you're right," she admitted quietly. "I'm sorry that I freaked out, but it really upsets me to see how unhappy Cathy is."

"We feel the same way, Ricki, but maybe it's just too soon."

Ricki stood up suddenly. "I think I'd like to ride back home now," she said quietly and began to untangle Diablo's snaffle. Kevin and Lillian got up, too, and fastened the bits to their animals.

Before Ricki could get back up into the saddle, however, she thought once more about the closeness of her friends.

"I'm sure Cathy will be herself again, in time," whispered Kevin tenderly into her ear, and kissed her softly in her hair.

"I sure hope so," replied Ricki. As she swung herself up into her horse's saddle and watched her friends do the same with theirs, she promised herself, despite all the dangers, to do everything she could to make Cathy remember how much Rashid had once meant to her. She just couldn't believe that Cathy had forgotten that feeling.

*

Cathy had calmed down a little. She turned the TV on again and stared at it as if in a trance, trying to figure out what had just happened. More than ever, she realized that her reaction was anything but normal.

You're crazy! The words thundered in her head. *You have really lost it!*

She tried to force herself to see the accident in her mind's eye, but just the idea was enough to make her tremble and sink into despair.

"Why?" she whispered hoarsely, tears running down her cheeks. "Why is this happening? Help me, this is driving me crazy!"

It's Rashid's fault! Only his fault! He's evil! All horses are bad! Bad, bad, bad! Cathy pressed both her hands over her ears in order to shut out the voice in her head.

"I . . . don't want to . . . hear. I . . . don't . . . want . . . to!" whispered the teenager, almost soundlessly to herself, and shook her head, as though she could drive out her thoughts. But it seemed to her that the inner voice became even louder.

RASHID IS BAD! IT'S HIS FAULT! You will never love another horse, because horses are bad, bad, bad! They make you scared, scared, scared!

"Noooooooooo!" Cathy howled. "I can't stand this any more!"

Abruptly, she got up and walked, as quickly as she could, out of her room and into the bathroom. She held her head under the faucet to try to shock herself into calmness with the cold running water.

"Would you please tell me what you're doing?" Bewildered, Mrs. Sutherland stared at her daughter, who bumped her head on the faucet when her mother startled her.

"Ow! You scared me! I thought you'd gone shopping!" Cathy, embarrassed, looked at her mother with red-rimmed eyes.

"Is everything okay?" asked Mrs. Sutherland suspiciously.

Cathy nodded, her hair soaking wet. "I . . . I just wanted to wash my hair," she lied, and was ashamed that she couldn't tell her mother the truth.

"Wash your hair? Didn't you just do that this morning?"

"I . . . no, I forgot to do it this morning!" Suddenly, the girl grabbed the shampoo bottle and poured some of the scented liquid onto her hair. For a few moments she could feel her mother's penetrating stare, but soon Cathy knew she was alone again, and she relaxed a little.

Exhausted, she sat down on the rim of the bathtub, as the shampoo foam wet her T-shirt. *I can't go on like this. I wish I knew what to do to keep these horrible panic attacks from coming back.*

Chapter 2

Ricki, Kevin and Lillian sat on the ground in front of the stable with their backs against the side of the building and let the sun shine on their faces. Rosie's puppies scrambled about them, vying for the best spots on the teens' laps.

Lillian, who was scratching Rosie behind her ears, laughed with delight. "They are so adorable! I could watch them play for hours!"

Kevin, who was trying to avoid the wet tongues of the gray puppies, turned his face away from one of them and asked his girlfriend, "Have you decided on names for the puppies yet? We can't just keep calling them, 'Hey you'!"

Ricki shook her head. "I can't make up my mind. There are so many possibilities. Do either of you have any suggestions?"

Lillian wrinkled her forehead and thought about it. "It would help to know how they're going to look when they grow up," she said as she watched the puppies at play. "What do you guys think? Will they look like Rosie?"

"No, I don't think so," Kevin answered. "Just look at

their fur. Rosie's is fairly short, but the puppies already have fur longer than their mother's."

"Too bad we don't know who the father is."

Kevin laughed out loud. "Lillian, do you think Ricki would demand child support if she knew?"

"With her sense of fairness, she just might," the sixteen-year-old played along with the joke, "but at least then we'd have a better idea of how the puppies will look when they grow up."

"I don't care who the father is," Ricki chimed in. "The main thing is that they are healthy and happy. I can't bear to think that I'll have to give them up soon."

"Yeah, that's really a bummer. But I've been working on my parents every day, and I hope they can be persuaded to take one. I've fallen in love with this little baby!" Lillian bent forward and pulled the puppy close to her.

"Baby? Baby wolf is more like it," grinned Kevin.

"A baby wolf. Hey, how about naming him Mowgli? You know, like the boy in *Jungle Book* who was raised by wolves."

"Mowgli?" Ricki looked at the puppy for a long time before she nodded enthusiastically. "I think the name fits him really well. Good! Mowgli it is."

Lillian beamed. "Now all we have to do is find great names for the other two. You'll see, it won't be that hard."

The friends were in a better mood, mostly because they weren't talking about Cathy.

"I got a D in math," said Ricki, changing the subject abruptly, and she glanced over at Kevin.

"Oh, your mother is going to be delighted!" grinned the boy. "How did you manage that?"

"Well, it was pretty difficult, always coming up with the wrong answer," responded Ricki. "What did you get?"

"Me? Didn't I already tell you at school? I have a glowing C!"

Ricki sighed. "Give me your C and I'll be the happiest person in the world. Mom has already threatened me with an after-school tutorial if my grades don't improve. I really don't feel like doing that."

"I wouldn't either, but what can you do?" Lillian blinked sleepily in the sun. "I've been having private lessons in Spanish for three months, but it hasn't really helped that much so far. It's not that I don't get it, I just don't want to take the language."

Ricki laughed. "Yeah, yeah, always an excuse! I'd like to see what would happen if I explained to my mother that I understand math well enough, but I just don't want to learn the subject, and that's why I get such bad grades. She'd probably lock me in a tower and auction Diablo off to the highest bidder! Up to now, I've been able to avoid having a tutor at home, but Mom's starting to make my life miserable. I can see myself now, sweating over the books on beautiful sunny days, while you two go riding and laugh yourselves silly over the idea of me sitting at home studying."

"You really think we'd do that, Ricki?" Lillian poked her friend in the ribs.

"Oh, all right! I take it all back! I'm sure you'd be crushed by my absence. By the way, what grade did Cathy get?"

"I'm not sure," Kevin said, "but from what I heard, a fairly good one. A or B, I think. She's always been good in math. Besides, she was keeping up with her lessons while she was recuperating at home, before she went back to school."

"Unbelievable! How does she do it?" Ricki shook her head in awe. Up until this year Ricki had been great at math, but lately there seemed to be so many distractions. Suddenly, she sat up and snapped her fingers. "Hey, I've got it!" she called out.

Kevin and Lillian jumped, startled, and gave her a quizzical look.

"What's gotten into you?"

"I think she's just had a math breakthrough."

Ricki grinned. "You could say that. I just decided to volunteer for extra math lessons, and Cathy will be my teacher."

Lillian exchanged a quick glance with Kevin. "Ricki, you have something else in mind, don't you? You don't really want to study math with Cathy, right? Admit it."

Ricki beamed. "What makes you say that?"

"Think about it. You don't want to make trouble for you or Cathy," said Kevin hesitantly, but his girlfriend just shrugged her shoulders.

"I'll learn math, and Cathy will learn something else. We'll tutor each other."

"Wow, you're pretty brave. Don't let Mother Sutherland catch you."

"Do you guys want to go visit Cathy? I have to ask her if she'll take me on as a pupil," said Ricki mischievously.

"Yeah, why not? But I don't feel like going anywhere afterward." Kevin got up lazily.

"Me neither!" Lillian held out her hand and let Kevin help her to her feet.

"Then let's get going!" added Ricki, and after the friends had said good-bye to the puppies, the three raced over to their bikes.

"Where are you off to?" called Brigitte Sulai, who was just coming out the door, carrying a laundry basket.

"We're going over to Cathy's for a while," her daughter answered, and the three of them got underway.

They hadn't gotten far from the house when a huge cloud of dust — a sure sign of Carlotta's car — appeared and enveloped them. Rashid's owner screeched her speeding car to a stop just in front of them.

"Hi, Carlotta!" Coughing, Ricki nodded to her. "Do you want to visit Rashid? He's fine. We took him with us on our ride this afternoon."

Carlotta smiled a little sadly. "Hello, you three. It's really nice of you to take my boy with you. Listen, I . . . well, a girl is going to come by the stable in a little while and take a look at Rashid. If the two of them get along, she's going to take over his care, instead of Cathy. I was just on my way to see your mother, Ricki, to tell her."

The kids' good moods vanished, and they stared at Carlotta in disbelief.

"You're not serious, are you?"

"A new girl? Who?"

"But what if, after all, Cathy —?"

Carlotta took a deep breath. "Please, don't make this more difficult for me than it already is! You all know that there's no one I'd rather have care for Rashid than Cathy, but you also know that you can't keep taking him with you, or riding him instead of your own horses."

"But —" Ricki was perplexed.

"If you're not gone too long, you'll be able to meet her. She's thirteen, and I've been told she's been riding for five years. I don't know anything else about her yet, but we'll see." Carlotta drove on quickly to put an end to the grilling. She was at least as miserable as the three kids, who felt that a new rider for Rashid would be seen as a betrayal of Cathy.

Their mouths open in astonishment, Ricki and her friends stared after Carlotta's car.

"She really did it."

"I never thought she would."

"But I suppose it was inevitable, and she's right, as far as Rashid is concerned." Ricki pounded the handlebars of her bike in anger and frustration. She just couldn't accept the fact that someone new would be coming to the stable to replace Cathy.

"Never!" she exclaimed, grinding her teeth. "You know what? You two should go back to the stable and meet the girl when she arrives. Maybe she won't like Rashid at all, or you'll realize that she just won't fit in with us, and then you can tell Carlotta. At any rate, don't leave the two of them alone in the stable. Listen in on the conversation, 'cause I want to know everything when I get back! I'm going to Cathy's." Ricki got back on her bike.

"Ricki, you aren't giving the girl Carlotta picked out any chance at all, and that's not fair. It's not her fault that everything turned out the way it has." Lillian looked straight into her friend's eyes. "Maybe she's really nice, and she'll get along great with Rashid and the rest of us."

Ricki bit her lip. "Yeah, I guess I'm not being fair, but

Cathy is our friend, and Rashid is simply *her* horse, and I don't want anyone to take her place. Ever!" With that, she pedaled away furiously, leaving Lillian and Kevin standing there. She had to talk with Cathy, one on one, as soon as possible, and make her understand, before Rashid was lost to her forever.

"Now what?" Kevin didn't feel comfortable with the situation.

"Let's ride back to the stable and look the new girl over. If she's really nice and gets along well with Rashid, then it will be our duty to tell Ricki something she doesn't want to hear. Oh, man, this won't be easy. I just hope Ricki doesn't do anything stupid!" groaned Lillian, and then the two of them pedaled back toward the stable.

*

"I'm looking at a horse today, and if all goes well, by tonight I'll have a horse to ride for free," announced the dark-haired teenager in the riding hall of the Avalon Riding Academy.

"Wow, how'd that happen? Who lets someone ride their horse without paying for it? And why doesn't stuff like that ever happen to me?" A little envious, Cheryl looked at her friend.

"The woman's name is Marconi, or something like that. My mother just happened to be answering the phone when the lady called to put an ad in the paper."

"Marconi? Isn't that the lady who's opening a ranch for sick and aging horses? I saw something about that in the paper a while ago."

"What?! Aging horses? Well, then, no thanks! I don't

want to ride some old neglected horse that's ready to be put down! If that's what this is about, then I don't think I'll bother to go after all." The dark-haired girl made a face.

"Oh, don't be like that. You should at least go and have a look."

"Yeah, and now I know why the riding won't cost anything. Worn-out nags . . . retired work horses . . . Who knows, they'd probably collapse if someone tried to sit on them!"

"Well, what are you going to do? Are you going there or not?" Cheryl wanted to know.

"I guess I have to. My mother made the appointment. Hey, want to come with me?"

Cheryl beamed. Secretly, she had hoped that her friend would invite her to come along. "Of course . . . if that's okay with you."

"Of course it's okay with me. After all, I may need someone to catch me if I faint at the sight of the old nag."

*

Exhausted, Ricki stood in front of the Sutherlands' front door, trying to catch her breath before she rang the doorbell. Her heart was beating wildly.

After a few minutes, the upstairs window to Cathy's bedroom opened, and her friend looked down at her.

"Oh, Ricki! Hold on a minute. I'm not moving too quickly these days, but I'll be right there!" called Cathy, and she hobbled gingerly down the stairs to open the door for Ricki. "Hey, it's great to see you. Come on in." She beamed, happy to see her friend. *Finally, a little distraction,* she thought.

"Hey, girlfriend! What's up? How was your day?" Ricki

28

tried to be as upbeat as possible as they went upstairs to Cathy's room.

"Well, it was okay. What did you guys do today? Oh, wait — I don't really want to know." Cathy stopped herself and ushered Ricki into her room. "Sit down. I bought a new CD yesterday. Want to hear it?" Without waiting for Ricki's answer, Cathy pulled a CD out from under a pile of magazines and put it into the player. Then she turned to her friend, and when she saw that Ricki was wearing her riding pants and boots, her expression hardened and she began to wring her hands anxiously. She couldn't take her eyes off Ricki's clothing.

"Something wrong?" asked Ricki as she noticed the fixed stare of her girlfriend.

"I —" Cathy turned around and covered her face with her hands.

"Hey, what's wrong?" Ricki shook her head, frightened, and jumped up to wrap her arms around her friend, but Cathy was as stiff as a board and tried to avoid Ricki's eyes.

"If you don't tell me what's wrong, I can't help you. Cathy, come on, start talking!"

"It's your clothes."

"My clothes? Oh, I forgot to change. So, it's my riding clothes that are up setting you?" Ricki realized, and Cathy jumped when she heard the word "riding." *My God,* thought Ricki, *this is really bad, and I thought —* Quickly she took a few steps backward and pulled off her riding pants and boots as fast as she could. Hurriedly, she hid the things behind a wide armchair, and then she breathed a sigh of relief and laid her hand on Cathy's shoulder.

"You can turn around again. I took that stuff off," she said softly and compassionately. She felt so sorry for Cathy, and she, who just a few moments before had been so sure that she could help her friend, now had no idea how she was going to do that.

Cathy, her eyes wet with tears, turned around and looked at her girlfriend. "I'm sorry . . . I can't help it. Please, forgive me," she said, stammering.

Ricki wrapped her arms tightly around her friend, and gave Cathy the opportunity, finally, to cry openly.

It took awhile for Cathy's tears to stop, and then the two of them sat down on the floor across from each other.

"I want to help you so much," said Ricki softly, "but I have no idea how to go about it."

Cathy sniffled loudly and looked at her friend. "No one can help me. I . . . I'm just plain crazy."

*

Lillian and Kevin were sorting out their grooming tools in the tack room and cleaning their brushes and currycombs when they heard unfamiliar voices coming from the stable, mixed with Carlotta's voice.

"Is it true that you have a ranch for retired and aging horses, Mrs. Marconi?"

"Well, at the moment, not really. Just the stalls have been renovated so far, but the ranch itself — I'm calling it Mercy Ranch — is still under construction," replied Carlotta, smiling, and then she thought of Jonah, who was still boarding at Lillian's parents' place. He would soon be coming to the ranch. "But there's already one saved horse."

30

Cheryl and her girlfriend exchanged a quick glance. The dark- haired girl shook her head firmly, but Carlotta hadn't noticed.

"Which one of you wants to ride?" Carlotta asked, directly.

The dark-haired girl impulsively pointed at Cheryl. "Cheryl! She's been looking for a horse to take care of for a long time, one that she can ride, too."

"What? Why are you —?" Cheryl looked at her girlfriend in astonishment, but the latter gave her a poke with her elbow to get her to stop talking.

"Come on, don't be like that. You've been talking about nothing else for weeks."

Lillian dropped the currycomb and it fell to the floor with a clatter. "Tell me it isn't true!" she whispered, and jumped up so that she could see through the window. She had recognized the voice immediately. "Sasha! Oh, no, Ricki will have a fit!"

"Well then, we're doomed!" replied Kevin in a whisper. "I think the best thing for us to do is disappear. Then we can say we —"

Carlotta and the two girls had almost reached the stall door.

"Yeah, well, I would really love the chance to ride," stammered Cheryl, while Sasha grinned spitefully.

"And you? Do you ride, too?" Carlotta turned to the dark-haired girl.

"Yes, but I already have a horse to care for," she lied.

"Since when?" The question slipped out of Cheryl and was met with a poisonous look from her girlfriend.

31

"Since . . . since yesterday. Didn't I tell you? And anyway, well, honestly, I wouldn't want to ride an old worn-out horse."

Carlotta stopped short and looked at the girl critically. "And why not? What's so bad about an old horse?"

"Oh, nothing really, except . . . that is . . . well, I can't really explain it, but like I said, I already have a horse to care for."

"I see!" Carlotta raised her eyebrows. If there was anything she couldn't stand, it was someone who thought that old or sick animals were worthless compared to young, fresh creatures.

"And how about you?" she asked warily, as her gaze wandered to Cheryl.

"I love all horses! I don't care if it's a Thoroughbred or a shaggy pony, a colt or a really old horse. I could hug all of them, and I think it's gross that there are people who have their horses put down just because they don't know what to do with them anymore," answered Cheryl, looking openly at Carlotta.

Rashid's owner sensed that this girl had a relationship to animals that was completely different from that of her friend, and suddenly everything became clear. This Sasha had thought that she was going to have to ride an old battered horse, and she had decided to let her friend do it instead.

Just you wait, thought Carlotta.

"Well good, then let's go have a look at the old boy. I hope you won't be too disappointed, Cheryl," she said as she led the two girls toward the stalls.

"No, no, Mrs. Marconi, absolutely not!" beamed Sasha's friend.

"Oh, by the way, my name is Mancini, not Marconi," grinned Carlotta, and Cheryl blushed bright red.

"Oops! I am soooo embarrassed! Sorry! I didn't mean anything by it. I thought —"

"That's okay. I just want to let you know. So, this is Rashid," she said casually, pointing at the dun horse, who raised his beautiful head when he heard his owner's voice and stretched his neck with the long rippling mane way over the edge of the stall.

"Wow, he's amazing!" Sasha burst out. And with shining eyes, she stared at the perfect dream horse.

"He's beautiful. I've never seen such a long mane." Cheryl was enchanted and stuck out her hand to touch the velvety soft nose.

Carlotta smiled proudly. "And next to him are Sharazan, Doc Holliday, and Diablo. The two little ones back there are Chico and Salina," she said, introducing Rashid's stable mates.

Sasha was startled. "Diablo? Isn't that Ricki Sulai's horse, and Doc Holliday —"

"Holli belongs to Lillian Bates. I remember him from back when he was boarded at the old riding stable," Cheryl completed the sentence for her girlfriend without taking her eyes off Rashid.

"Hi, Sasha! Hello, Cheryl!" Lillian and Kevin came out of the tack room, one behind the other.

"Hey! I didn't know that you boarded your horses at Mercy Ranch," said Sasha, and she frowned.

"Mercy Ranch?" Kevin looked over at Carlotta.

"Well, Mrs. Mar — ah, Mancini said that —"

"Me?" Carlotta laughed. "I didn't say this is Mercy Ranch! This young lady here thinks that the riding opportunity is for one of the retired horses."

"Really?" Kevin began to grin broadly, and Lillian had to fight to stop from giggling.

Unnerved, Sasha looked from one to the other. Somehow she didn't feel so sure of herself anymore.

On the other hand, Cheryl had obviously fallen in love with Rashid, and scratched him on his favorite spot, just behind his ears.

"Oh, he is so sweet! Yes, you are really a sweetheart, aren't you?" she whispered to him softly, and Carlotta nodded approvingly.

"Well, since Sasha has let it be known that she doesn't want to ride old nags, she has, if I'm not mistaken, gotten her friend to take her place."

"Oh, wow." Kevin slapped his thigh. "That is some joke! That's great!"

"That . . . that's not true. I just —" stammered Sasha, unable to finish the sentence.

"Whatever!" Carlotta said in her best teenager imitation as she put her hand on Cheryl's shoulder. "Young lady, I think you're perfect for my horse!"

The girl was really pleased by Carlotta's praise. She threw Rashid a good-bye look, and stepped back, sighing.

"And where's the horse that you're letting me ride?" she asked, her heart beating wildly.

Lillian grinned even more broadly. "Well, Cheryl, you can hardly miss him, can you?"

"What do you mean?"

"Well, Rashid is pretty huge, isn't he?" Kevin leaned casually against Sharazan's stall.

"Rashid?" At first, Cheryl turned pale, then red, and she had the feeling that she was so happy she would faint. "Rashid is the horse that needs a rider? Nooo, that's unreal! Mrs. Mancini, is that really true? You're letting me take care of Rashid, and ride him?"

Carlotta nodded sweetly. "You've been riding for a while, haven't you?" she asked, just to be on the safe side.

Cheryl nodded enthusiastically. "Yes, for four years!"

"Then okay. You know what, you can take him out of the stall, groom, saddle him, and ride him around a bit, so I can see how you two get along. If Rashid is satisfied with you, then I will be too."

Cheryl still couldn't believe her luck. "I don't know what to say. That is . . . that is just . . . oh, Sasha, why don't you say something?"

"That is just . . . garbage!" exploded the dark-haired girl, furious with herself. Sasha stormed outside, jumped on her bike and rode off as though she were being chased. Kevin and Lillian's laughter still sounded like mockery in her ears.

*

"You should have seen her speeding away!" jeered Kevin as he gave Ricki a report on his cell phone.

"And Cheryl is riding Rashid, right now?"

"Yeah! And you know what? The two of them really do seem to get along well!"

A less than enthusiastic "Terrific!" was all Ricki could

say. She was silent as she thought of Cathy, who had just left the room for a few minutes.

"Are you still there?" asked Kevin when he didn't hear anything more from his girlfriend.

"The . . . the connection is breaking up." Ricki told a white lie because she didn't want to talk anymore. "See you later." Abruptly, she ended the call.

What a mess! she thought. *Rashid gets along perfectly with the new girl, Cathy is forgotten, and the worst part of it is that Cheryl is really nice.* Ricki turned off her new cell phone and waited for Cathy to return.

Cathy, who had almost had the doorknob in her hand, had inadvertently overheard Ricki's telephone conversation.

Cheryl is riding Rashid? At these words, Cathy felt panic again. Something strange was happening to her, something she couldn't explain. A feeling of jealousy was rising within her, but what could she be jealous of? Rashid. The mere mention of that name brought out a cold sweat on Cathy's brow.

"No, I want this to stop! I'm . . . I'm . . . fine!" Cathy said aloud.

"Cathy? What are you doing? I thought you went to . . ." Ricki, who wanted to find out what had upset her friend, wrapped her arm around her and led her back into the room.

Darn, she thought. *She must have heard me on the phone. Oh, I'm such an idiot! But I couldn't have known that she was standing just outside the door.*

"Cathy, I'm home!" called Mrs. Sutherland as she stuck her head in Cathy's room. When she saw her daughter's ash-gray face, she pushed the door open so forcibly that it banged against the wall.

"Hello, Mrs. Sutherland," Ricki dared to say, but the angry, bitter look that struck her made her retreat.

"What did you do to my daughter? Did you talk to her about things that I have forbidden to be mentioned?" exploded Mrs. Sutherland. Ricki lowered her head and stared at the floor.

"GET OUT!" Cathy's mother shoved the girl out the door. "And don't even think about coming back here again! It was irresponsible, whatever you did! GET OUT! Do you hear me?"

Ricki took one more look at Cathy, who looked at her with sad eyes pleading for forgiveness. Then she left the room quickly, ran down the stairs, and breathed a sigh of relief when she had slammed the door shut behind her.

As she went to get on her bike, she realized that all she had on was her T-shirt, underpants, and socks, and she was standing in the middle of the road, shivering. Mrs. Sutherland hadn't even given her time to get dressed again.

"Oh, no!" she groaned in desperation. "What now? My riding clothes are in Cathy's room. What am I going to do? I can't ride home like this." She was about to ring the doorbell, when Mrs. Sutherland threw open the door.

"I guess these belong to you! Now get going, and don't you ever come back here again!" she yelled at Ricki, throwing her riding pants and boots at her feet, followed by her jacket.

Ricki's face turned red, and she got dressed as quickly as she could.

"Ricki . . . Ricki," Cathy called to her girlfriend in a miserable soft voice from her window. "I am so sorry. Please, Ricki, don't be mad."

If I could just get these darn boots on . . . Ricki tried hard and finally she made it. Sadly, she glanced up at Cathy.

"No problem," she assured her and hoped that Mrs. Sutherland wouldn't appear again. She was just about to turn and ride off, but turned back.

"Cathy, you'll see, you'll make it!" she called to her girlfriend, but Cathy just shook her head slowly.

"Yes, you will, Cathy! You'll make it! You were able to look at me the whole time just now, even though I had riding clothes on. See, it doesn't bother you. Hey, I love you! No matter what your mother thinks of me, you have to know that I'm on your side. We'll see each other later at school!" Ricki sent a smile up to Cathy.

Cathy stared incredulously at Ricki and felt like her heart had turned a cartwheel.

"She's right," Cathy whispered to herself. Slowly, she went back into her room. She walked hesitantly toward her bookcase. On the top shelf there was a large illustrated book about the different breeds of horses. Cathy swallowed. Did she dare to pull that book out and look at it? But just the thought of horses made her tremble again, and she gave up, disappointed. But for a moment at least, she actually believed that she had overcome her fear.

Chapter 3

After a brief ride on Rashid on the paddock, during which she was closely watched by Carlotta, Lillian, and Kevin, Cheryl brought the gelding back to the stable and worked hard to dry off his sweaty coat and brush it smooth again. Jake stood beside her and, with an expert eye, watched her work.

"You're doing a good job," he commented as Cheryl put Rashid back in his stall. The old stable hand went outside, a broad grin on his face, to give the thumbs-up sign. *She's okay with me,* was the obvious message.

"Well, now that we know what Jake thinks of her, what do you two think?" Carlotta asked, leaning against her car.

Lillian and Kevin were puzzled by her question. Could it be that Carlotta was going to leave the decision up to the two of them?

"Well, Cheryl is really nice, and it looks like she gets along well with Rashid," began Lillian slowly, "but —"

"But what?"

"Well . . . " Kevin struggled a little too. "It's just that

we . . . we have to get used to the idea that Cathy won't be looking after Rashid anymore."

"Kids, we've already talked about this, and you know how I feel. The only thing I want to know from you at the moment is if you could accept Cheryl here in this stable as Rashid's new rider. If that doesn't work, then she could be the best rider in the world and could get along perfectly with Rashid, and she still wouldn't be happy here. So, you two, what's it going to be? But before you answer, I want to ask you to be fair."

Lillian nodded. "Well, I think we'll get along okay with Cheryl, don't you, Kevin?"

"Yeah, I think so too. But I don't know about Ricki —"

Carlotta dismissed his worries. "If you two can get along with Cheryl, I'm sure Ricki will too. And the main thing is that she gets along well with Rashid, right? Well, I'm going to tell her the good news," she said, winking. She limped over to the stable on her crutches, which had been her constant companions for years, ever since she'd had a serious riding accident in her circus-performing days.

A moment later, Cheryl appeared, her face beaming. "You can't imagine how happy I am," she called to them excitedly.

Lillian swallowed, but then she smiled, too. "Well, then, welcome to the club! I hope we'll have a lot of wonderful rides together," she responded, and Kevin nodded in agreement.

"The only bad thing about this is now I'll have to deal with three girls again," he grinned.

"What do you mean, 'again'?" Cheryl wanted to know, but the boy shook his head.

"We'll tell you about it someday."

"Okay. I have to leave now, unfortunately. Is it all right if I come back tomorrow?" asked Cheryl.

"Come as often as you like. Rashid really needs the exercise," exclaimed Carlotta. "All I need now is a written release from your parents explaining that they have given their permission for you to ride and take care of Rashid."

"Of course! That's no problem! I'll bring it tomorrow. When are you usually in the stable?"

Lillian thought it over. "Actually, we don't have a fixed time, but we're usually here every afternoon, when we're finished with our homework."

"Good. Then I'll see you tomorrow afternoon. And thank you so much, Mrs. Mancini!"

"You're welcome, Cheryl. I'm glad to have found such a good rider so quickly, and it's obvious that Rashid feels comfortable with you," grinned Carlotta as she headed for her car. "Take care, Kevin, Lillian, and say hello to Ricki for me."

"Will do. Good-bye, Carlotta!"

"So long!"

"Good-bye, Mrs. Mancini!" called Cheryl. "And I'll see you guys tomorrow, okay?" she said to the others as she rode off on her bike, her heart pounding with excitement. Cheryl's thoughts stayed with Rashid for a long time. Then she remembered Sasha.

Oh, no, she thought. *She's going to be really ticked off, but it's her own fault that it turned out like this.*

*

"Come on, Ricki, don't make that face. Cheryl is okay. Really." Lillian sat opposite her friend on the Sulais'

41

couch and tried to start a conversation, but Ricki's thoughts were elsewhere.

"Sorry, what did you just say?" she asked guiltily, absentmindedly picking out the red M&Ms from the bowl on the coffee table.

"Lillian said that Cheryl is really nice," repeated Kevin.

"Oh, yeah."

"Hey, Ricki, you haven't said anything about how it went with Cathy. Is she going to tutor you or not?" Lillian wanted to know, but Ricki just shrugged her shoulders.

"I have no idea. We didn't talk about it."

"But that's why you went there in the first place, isn't it? Hey, don't make this so difficult. What did she say? How is she?" There was nothing Kevin hated more than getting incomplete answers to his questions.

Ricki sighed. "She's not doing well at all. She had a panic attack when she heard Rashid's name, while I was on the phone with you, and if you had seen how she reacted to my riding clothes —! But that's another story."

"You are going to tell us, aren't you?" Lillian asked.

"I don't know, it's a little embarrassing."

"Don't make such a big thing out of this. Come on, talk!"

"Okay." Ricki began hesitantly, but then everything just burst out. Before she'd even finished, Kevin exploded with laughter.

"You were what? Standing in your underwear in the street? I wish I'd seen that!"

Lillian giggled with him. "Typical Ricki!" she said, but her girlfriend just ignored her.

"You know what, I really don't care about that now.

When I'd finished getting dressed and was standing under Cathy's window, and she was looking down at me, suddenly she could stand to look at me — riding clothes and all — without bursting into tears!"

"Well, yeah, Ricki, your appearance does tend to make people cry!" Kevin was still laughing.

"Get serious!" Ricki frowned angrily. "Don't you get what I'm saying? When I got there, Cathy freaked out when she saw my riding clothes, but when I left, she could look at me without getting upset. And that was worth all the embarrassment!"

Lillian finally understood. "Hey, you're right! That's a sure sign that somebody really could work with Cathy to help her get over her fear, if —"

"— If Mrs. Sutherland doesn't ruin everything!"

"Exactly!"

Suddenly Kevin didn't feel like laughing anymore.

"Does that woman know what she's doing to Cathy with her stupid behavior, or doesn't she want to know?" he asked.

"I think she doesn't want to know. After all, she was never in favor of Cathy riding," answered Lillian, and Ricki agreed with her.

"I'm overloaded on this topic for the day. My brain is now officially fried. Can we change the subject?" asked Ricki as she rubbed her eyes, tired.

"Well, do you want to hear more about Cheryl and Rashid?"

"No, not really," admitted Ricki. "Oh, I don't know what I want. Maybe a ride on Diablo will clear my head."

"I've got an idea," said Lillian. "Let's go to the movies."

"Oh, yeah! What's playing?" Kevin was enthusiastic. "Ricki, do you have the paper with the movie schedule?"

"No, but there's sure to be everything from a romantic tear-jerker to a gory action film."

"Probably. So, people, what do you think? Do you feel like going?" Lillian looked from one to the other.

"I'll go," responded Kevin.

Ricki nodded. "Okay, but if I fall asleep and start to snore, you two have to carry me home."

"That's no problem," Lillian grinned. "C'mon, let's get changed and go downtown. If we're early, we can let Josh buy us some ice cream."

"Girls! You're always getting your boyfriends to pay!" Kevin pretended to be annoyed.

"Oh, Kevin, thank you! That is so nice of you to invite me to the movies!" Ricki took his arm and beamed at him.

"Uh . . . that's not exactly what I meant."

"No? Too bad. Well, it was worth a try anyway."

*

"Come on, Sasha, don't be so mad," pleaded Cheryl. "After all, it was your idea to suggest me for this riding thing."

"Yeah, I know. But you don't have to keep telling me about how wonderful Rashid is!"

Cheryl took a deep breath. When her friend was in a bad mood, you couldn't really talk to her.

"Maybe I could talk to Mrs. Mancini about it. Maybe we could share Rashid," she suggested, but Sasha shook her head.

"Forget about it. You don't think she would ever let me ride Rashid after what I said about old horses. Oh, I was so stupid. I really messed up everything!"

"Yeah, thank goodness!" burst out Cheryl, and got a nasty look from her friend. "Sorry, but —"

"Can't you just be quiet?"

Cheryl sighed loudly. "Would it cheer you up if I invited you to the movies?" she asked, trying to get back into Sasha's good graces.

"Hmm," she growled, and swayed back and forth angrily.

"Is that a yes or a no?" Cheryl pressed her.

"I guess so," answered Sasha, bored.

"Then let's go, or the movie will start without us. Do you think they'll throw me out if I go wearing my riding stuff?" asked Cheryl, grinning mischievously.

"Maybe, and then I'll just have to tell you how the movie was," came the self-centered answer from her friend.

*

"Wow, that flick was really great! The way that guy went galloping through the woods, with all those men following him . . . really wild," raved Lillian as she put the last few pieces of popcorn into her mouth.

"I don't know why you two always rave about the guys. I thought the little blonde girl in the hut was much more interesting," grinned Kevin, which earned him a poke in the ribs from Ricki.

"Well, just don't expect me to bleach my hair!" she said. She didn't like it when Kevin raved about other girls in front of her, especially when they were as good looking as the young actress in the film.

"Oh, come on. You know I like you just the way you are," Kevin assured his girlfriend, giving her a big kiss on the cheek.

"Yuck! You're all sticky and salty from the popcorn," responded Ricki, wiping her cheek as they left the theater.

"So what is . . ." began Lillian.

"Hey! Did you guys see the movie, too?" Cheryl, who was suddenly standing behind them with Sasha, interrupted Lillian in mid sentence.

"Oh, hello! Looks like we have the same taste — and not just in horses," answered Kevin, smiling at Rashid's new rider.

Lillian nodded to her too. "Hi, Cheryl! What a nice surprise!"

Ricki didn't know how to react, but she reached out her hand to Cheryl. "Hello there, I'm Ricki Sulai. Do you remember me from the riding academy? We haven't seen much of each other lately."

"Sure, of course I remember you, Ricki. I've always been jealous of your fabulous horse. I saw him today. He's even more beautiful than I remember him!" Cheryl shook Ricki's hand firmly which, along with her Diablo compliment, won Ricki over immediately.

She's really nice, Ricki thought. *I wonder if she'll stay that way.*

"Oh! Now you're suddenly good friends! Hey, Cheryl, didn't you say you thought Ricki was a total snob and weird, because she never lets anyone but her ride Diablo? Hi, by the way!" Sasha gave them a phony smile, while Cheryl turned bright red.

"That's not true! Why did you say that?" The girl shook her head slowly and stared incredulously at her friend.

Ricki raised one eyebrow, which made her look a little arrogant, and glanced back and forth between Cheryl and Sasha.

46

Lillian decided to take over and, smiling broadly, shot back, "Hey, Sasha. I didn't see you. That's a really interesting bit of information. Why don't you tell us more?"

Cheryl turned pale and looked at the three friends, horrified. Sasha was about to ruin everything before it had even begun.

"Don't hold back, Sasha. We're all ears," said Kevin, nodding encouragingly.

"Well," Sasha smiled haughtily. "First of all, Cheryl doesn't like black horses, and secondly, when Diablo's former owner whipped him, she said that Diablo deserved what he got, because he —"

"Excuse me, but I have to interrupt you for a sec. Could it be that you're trying to mess up your friend's chances with us because Mrs. Mancini chose her to ride Rashid?" suggested Lillian, looking the dark-haired girl directly in the eyes.

Ricki took a step toward Sasha. "Has anyone ever told you you're a terrible liar, Sasha Bolton? Cheryl couldn't have said those things. She doesn't know anything about Diablo!" Ricki's eyes sparkled furiously. "I have to wonder, though, why did Cheryl decide to choose you as a friend? You don't deserve her, the way you talk about her!"

"Oh, yeah? Well, as far as I'm concerned, you can have her! She's boring anyway, and completely beneath me!" Sasha turned and started to walk away proudly, her head held high, but Ricki's voice held her back.

"It would be impossible for anyone to be beneath you!" she called after her, before she turned back to Cheryl, who had tears in her eyes.

47

"I think you've just lost a friend, but at least now you've got three new ones," she said softly. "Hey, the three of us are going riding tomorrow afternoon. Would you like to come with us, or would you rather practice for a few days on the paddock?"

"You . . . you don't believe those things Sasha said about me, do you?" Cheryl asked nervously.

"Of course not. Most of what she says is just idiotic anyway. Anyone who likes her has to be insane. Oh, sorry, I didn't really mean that the way it sounded," stammered Lillian, but Cheryl had already begun to laugh.

"You're right! But she was the first kid I met when we moved here, and we just became friends. Oh, I am so excited about tomorrow! Of course I'll go riding with you. I trust Rashid one hundred percent!"

"Pssst," said Lillian and pointed to the left.

"Oh, no, it's Cathy! What's she doing here?" Ricki had just spotted her girlfriend, who had been standing with her back to them.

"Is Rashid actually a —?"

"Be quiet!" Kevin broke into Cheryl's next sentence.

"And there's Mrs. Sutherland, coming to pick her up. Let's get out of here before she sees me!" Ricki ran off a few yards, followed by the others.

"What's going on?" asked Cheryl, bewildered. She didn't understand why they were running away from this girl.

"We'll tell you later, but first we have to get out of here!"

"Will you please tell me *now* what's going on?" Cheryl asked and looked at the others expectantly.

"Okay, listen closely," said Kevin and started to tell her the story of Rashid and Cathy.

*

Cathy got into her mother's car and brooded in silence. She had seen her friends, too, in the movie theater, but because she didn't want to get Ricki into any more trouble, she had turned her back to them and pretended not to see them. After all, her mother would be there any minute to pick her up.

That was how she inadvertently overheard the conversation between her friends and Sasha and Cheryl, and was startled when she heard Rashid's name.

She wanted to flee, to get away from her memories of the accident, but something held her back.

Was it because of Sasha, who was always trying to be the center of attention by making up stories? Or was it because of Cheryl, who, all of sudden, was acting as though she had been friends with Ricki and the others forever?

Cathy closed her eyes and pressed herself firmly into the front seat of the car. The feeling that she was being excluded from her circle of friends devastated her.

"The movie must not have been very good, judging by your face," commented Mrs. Sutherland after a brief glance at her daughter.

"Hmm," responded Cathy, without paying any attention to her mother. Hadn't she heard Ricki say something about a new friendship? With Cheryl?

And then Cathy remembered a few scraps of the conversation that she'd tried to ignore, since they had to do with Rashid. *Of course, I'll go riding with you! I trust Rashid one hundred percent!* Cathy clenched her teeth to rid herself of the goose bumps she got just thinking about Rashid. What made things even worse was the feeling that she, Cathy, was now completely out of the picture. Just like that! Without consulting her, Carlotta had replaced her with Cheryl! Cheryl would be the one who would be meeting with Ricki, Lillian, and Kevin at the stable in the future and who would be having fun with them, and Cathy would gradually be forgotten!

Cathy groaned softly. *And I always thought Cheryl was so nice! How can she do this to me? She's taking my friends away from me! And she's taking Rashid away from me!* The girl sensed anger rising in her. *I hate you, Cheryl Vincent! You and Ricki and Lillian and Kevin. You all just got rid of me! That is so mean! And it hurts soooo much!*

*

"Hey, Cathy, what's up?" Ricki locked her bike and pulled her book bag out of the bike basket. She walked toward her friend, in a good mood, but Cathy just looked at her with a strange, blank face.

"Is something wrong?" asked Ricki, but Cathy turned away abruptly.

"What could be wrong?" Grumpily, Cathy threw her backpack over her shoulder and walked toward the school entrance without saying another word.

"What was that all about?" Kevin stopped his bike in front of Ricki.

"I really don't know," the girl said, shrugging her shoulders. "Hey, it's not like we're always in a good mood either. Maybe she didn't sleep well."

"Good morning, everybody!" grinned Lillian as she jumped down from her bike. "Everything all right?"

"With us, yeah!" replied Ricki.

"What's that supposed to mean?"

"Well, Cathy seems to have gotten up on the wrong side of the bed this morning."

"Oh, it happens." Lillian glanced at her watch. "Oops, people, I think we'd better get a move on. We're already a little late!"

The friends ran into the school in an attempt to make it to their classes on time.

"See ya!" called Lillian, leaving the two others and running into her classroom.

Ricki and Kevin breathed a sigh of relief as they reached their seats before the bell rang.

"Just made it!" grinned Ricki to Cathy, and collapsed, mock-exhausted, on the chair beside her. "Hey, do you have the corrections on the math exam? I wanted to do it yesterday, but I just don't get it. Can I copy them from you?" Ricki asked batting her eyes pleadingly.

"No!" Cathy slammed her English book and the notebook for the next class down onto her desk.

"No?" asked Ricki, bewildered.

"You asked me something and I said NO!" was Cathy's abrupt answer.

Ricki shook her head as though she had water in her ears. "Why not? Didn't you do them either?" She gave her a friendly poke, but Cathy just leaned away from her.

"Of course I have the corrections!"

"Then could you please at least explain to me how to do

them? I wanted to ask you yesterday if you would tutor me in —"

"No!"

"Hey, Cathy, what's wrong with you? Did I do something to make you angry? If I did, then tell me please, because I just don't know what it is!"

"Oh, just leave me alone, okay? Go get some other idiot to copy from. I'm tired of it. And you can forget about the tutoring thing. I have better things to do," Cathy spat back at her.

"Well, thanks a lot for being so nice about it," Ricki said with sarcasm, then glanced over at Kevin, a puzzled expression on her face. But before Ricki could give Cathy's strange behavior any further thought, Mr. Reid, the substitute English teacher, came into the room.

"Good morning, everyone," he announced pleasantly. "How'd you all like a surprise grammar quiz?"

The class groaned loudly, and Mr. Reid beamed.

"I just knew you'd love the idea. So, let's go. Get your notebooks out and we can begin."

Chapter 4

"That was really mean of you yesterday," Cheryl said to Sasha during lunch break.

"Why? What'd I do?" Sasha asked, faking innocence.

"How can you even ask that? You lied about me, and about having a horse of your own to ride and look after!"

"So what?" replied Sasha icily.

"Can I help it if you're stupid enough to mess up an opportunity to ride a fabulous horse?"

"Fabulous horse? Don't make me laugh. That's not how I would describe him."

"Oh? Well, that's interesting, considering your mouth dropped wide open when you saw him," replied Cheryl, furious.

"Why are you getting so upset? You've only seen Ricki a few times and you're already acting as though you're best friends! Have you ever considered how that could hurt my feelings? Who was always there for you when you first moved here and didn't know anyone? Was it Ricki?"

"No! That was you, but that doesn't give you the right to spread lies about me! That hurts *my* feelings!"

"Oh, really!" Sasha turned aside a bit and noticed Ricki, Kevin, and Lillian, who were standing on the other side of the school grounds and seemed to be engaged in a serious discussion with Cathy.

"Listen! If there's something about me that you don't like, then why don't you go over to them? They suit you better anyway. They're just as childish as you are." She pointed vaguely in another direction, but Cheryl knew immediately whom she meant.

"That's exactly what I'm going to do, Sasha. And in the future, just stay away from me. I don't want to have anything more to do with a liar like you!"

"Terrific! That clears up everything. I'll be glad to be rid of you. There are way cooler kids to hang out with." Sasha smiled her snobby little smile and pranced away.

"Well, that's the end of that!" Cheryl said. As she began to walk toward her new riding friends she overheard a loud argument that ended abruptly when Cathy noticed Cheryl.

"I don't care about any of you!" was the last thing Cathy said as she rushed past Rashid's new rider without a word of greeting.

"Did I interrupt something?" asked Cheryl, looking after Cathy nervously.

"No, not at all. She's being impossible today. She's totally messed up." Ricki's face was still a little pink.

"What's wrong with her?"

"It seems as though she's jealous of you, Cheryl," answered Kevin.

"But why? I mean . . . I thought that after the accident she was afraid of Rashid anyway?"

"Apparently that's just one of many problems. She thinks that now that you're Rashid's designated rider we won't want to be friends with her anymore," Lillian tried to explain.

"Uh-oh, that's not good," responded Cheryl. "Do you think it would help if I talked to her?"

"Don't do that to yourself, at least not today," warned Ricki. "When Cathy's in a mood like this, it's better to stay away from her. I think we have to get going. I'll be so glad when school is over for the day. So, Cheryl, see you later this afternoon at the stable."

"Okay. I'm really looking forward to it. Later!"

"Yep. So long!"

*

Ricki and her friends were already on their way home when Sasha stopped Cathy in front of the school.

"Hey, Cathy! Ricki and Company have already left," she said, grinning.

"So?"

"I just meant that usually you all go home together."

Cathy fastened her backpack onto her bike rack and started to leave without saying anything. She didn't feel like talking to Sasha, especially not about her former friends.

"Did you guys have a fight?" Sasha probed deeper, but Cathy still didn't react. "It was because of Cheryl, wasn't it?"

"Yeah, because of Cheryl. But what business is that of yours?" Cathy replied gruffly.

"I heard that she's riding that horse now . . . the one you had your accident with . . . and I thought right away that you wouldn't like that."

55

Cathy turned pale. All she wanted was to get away from Sasha.

"I couldn't care less if she rides him. Just leave me alone! I don't feel like talking to you about it." She tugged her bike out of the bike stand and got on quickly.

"Cheryl isn't friends with me anymore because I didn't think it was good that —"

"Sasha, I want you to leave me ALONE!"

"— and she told me that you are out of the group now that she's riding with them," added Sasha, ignoring her.

"WHAT?" Suddenly, Cathy was all ears. "She said that?"

"Yeah. Today at lunch."

"Well, that's just great," Cathy said, stunned.

"Isn't it? What kind of friends can they be if they drop you so quickly?"

Cathy swallowed hard. Sasha had said exactly what Cathy had been thinking.

"If you want, you can talk to me," offered Sasha smugly, but Cathy just shook her head before she rode off.

I will never talk to you about that — or anything else, she thought, as the wind dried her tears.

*

"Hey, Lillian, Carlotta just called to ask if we feel like riding over to her ranch and helping out at the stable." Ricki was getting into Diablo's saddle, waiting for the rest of her friends to saddle up.

"The stable? Does that mean that some horses are arriving tomorrow?" Lillian wanted to know.

"No, not yet, but in the next few days for sure, she said.

And she also said that I should tell you that your father can bring Jonah anytime between now and the weekend, whenever he wants."

Lillian sighed deeply. "Oh, no, my father's going to be really sad. He's gotten so used to that sweetie, and I'm going to miss him, too. Oh, well, we always knew that he was staying with us only until Carlotta's ranch was ready. And we don't have a real horse stable for him anyway."

"But Lily, we know where he's going, and Jonah will be just as happy there as he was at your place. Ready?" Kevin looked around at everyone and smiled at Cheryl, who had just swung up into Rashid's saddle, her face pink with excitement and happiness.

"People, you wouldn't believe how happy I am!" she said, beaming. "Do you know how long it's been since I got to go trail riding? It feels like about a hundred years. Our new riding instructor won't let us leave the ring very often."

"Rashid is great in the fields. Cathy's accident would never have happened if that stupid hot-air balloon hadn't been there and frightened Rashid with the hissing of the burner. And even then, probably nothing would have happened if Cathy had been secure in the saddle. It's just that her appendix burst just then," commented Lillian, trying to make Cheryl understand that she didn't have anything to worry about when she was riding the dun horse.

Cheryl laughed happily. "Not to worry. I'm not afraid, if that's what you mean."

"Well, okay then! Let's go to Carlotta's ranch. She's expecting us."

Each in a good mood, the friends guided their horses out

of the yard, and it was clear that Rashid was very happy to be going along with the others, and to have someone riding him again.

"Did you know that Sharazan and Rashid were circus horses before we got them?" Kevin asked Cheryl, who shook her head amazed.

"No, tell me about it."

"Well, it was like this . . . "

*

Carlotta limped back and forth in the kitchen of her ranch house. She had the telephone to her ear, and she was frowning and seemed extremely upset.

"No, you just can't . . . where are they? And how long has that been going on? I see, uh-huh . . . and why . . . ? Uh-huh! . . . Are you crazy? I can't change the whole ranch opening, these things take time . . . What? . . . if I can pick up the animal today? How? My horse trailer won't be here until the beginning of next week! But . . . What? . . . Yes, I'll definitely drive over there. Tell them I'm on my way. Good! Yes, I'll call you back! Yes, today! Good-bye!" Carlotta let the receiver drop. *It's already starting*, she thought, furious. *As soon as word was out that I'm opening a ranch for aging horses, the calls started coming in from people who are just tired of their horses. I can't believe owners threaten to put them down if I don't accept them here! It's awful!*

She poured herself a mug of coffee and went to the window, where she could see Ricki and the others on their horses in the distance.

"If only everybody had the same relationship to animals

58

as those four young people do, then the world would be a much safer place for animals," Carlotta sighed softly as she plopped down on the chair and waited for the kids to arrive.

*

I wonder if I should call Sasha after all? thought Cathy as she paced back and forth in her room. *She did offer, and if the others don't want to have anything to do with me anymore, then . . .* Cathy stood in front of her bookshelves and she noticed the large illustrated book about the different breeds of horses.

She stared at it for a long time, torn about what to do, and then she reached out her hand tentatively to pull it out. Her hands were trembling.

"I want to look at it!" she pleaded with herself in a soft, quivering voice. "It's not normal that I can't even look at the pictures anymore. Maybe . . . maybe everything would be different, if I had gone to see Rashid myself, after —" Cathy swallowed, and then she began to think about Cheryl. Immediately she was overwhelmed with anger.

"You . . . you nasty little rat! You stole my friends and my horse," she hissed, furious, and tore the book off the shelf, opened it up, and forced herself to look at the wonderful purebred stallion on the page.

"I'll make it! I'll show all of you! None of you have any faith in me, and you have no idea how much that hurts!" Cathy hurled the book into the corner of the room and threw herself onto the bed, sobbing. "And Sasha will be a good friend, at least a better one than I've had up to now, Ricki Sulai!"

"Hello! There you are. I'm so glad you came!" Carlotta waved to the riders.

"Gee, Carlotta, it looks really great around here," Ricki said, looking around.

"That's true! I had some good helpers here who tidied up the chaos in the yard quickly, and let me tell you, it was about time that things got organized around here. How was your ride? Everything okay, Cheryl?"

"Thanks, Mrs. Mancini. Rashid is a wonderful horse. The ride was marvelous!" The girl beamed as she stroked Rashid's neck affectionately.

Carlotta nodded kindly at her. "Well, then, that's good. By the way, did you remember the permission slip from your parents?" she asked.

Cheryl nodded and stuck her hand into the woven bag she was wearing over her shoulder. "Just a sec, let me grab it. Oops, it's a little wrinkled," she grinned apologetically, pulling it out.

"As long as I can read what it says, I don't care about a few wrinkles," laughed Carlotta as she took the paper and scanned it. "Good. Everything's okay. From now on, as far as I'm concerned, you can ride Rashid whenever you want. Except for night rides or participating in events. If you're planning anything like that, then please talk to me about it beforehand."

"I will. I am so happy! I never in a million years thought that I'd have such a great riding opportunity."

"Well, there you go. You see how fast something can happen," laughed Kevin.

"Okay. Listen up, people! You can unsaddle the horses and put them over there on the paddock so that the animals can relax while you're helping me with the stalls. Okay?" Carlotta pointed to a large newly fenced-in meadow.

"No prob!" Lillian jumped down from Holli's back and started to loosen the saddle girth.

"Wait, I'll bring you some halters," announced Carlotta, but Ricki gave her Diablo's reins.

"Where are they?"

"In the tack room, to the right, on top of the cupboard." Ricki was already on her way.

"When are the first horses going to arrive?" asked Kevin as he took off Diablo's and Sharazan's saddles.

"Actually, I thought that it was going to start next week, but I just got a call. Hmm, let's see — Ah, here comes Ricki. Did you find them?"

Ricki answered by holding up four brand-new halters.

"They're great! Did you buy them at Josh's father's shop?"

Carlotta shook her head and laughed. "No. Someone gave them to me."

"How did you manage that? I wouldn't mind that kind of present." Ricki distributed the halters.

"Don't tell me you're complaining. Didn't you get a beautiful saddle blanket from Josh, with Diablo's name on it in gold?" Lillian poked her friend hard.

"Yeah, but it was my birthday and it isn't Carlotta's birthday," the girl defended herself.

"Maybe we should take the arrival of the horses here at the ranch as their birthday, starting a new life. Then it would be a present for the horses, not for Mrs. Mancini," commented Cheryl, and Carlotta nodded.

"That's exactly what Josh's father said, and he promised me he would give each new horse a halter. He's also giving me grooming tack, horse shampoo, and a few other useful items."

"Wow! That's really nice of him!"

"Yes, it is. So, when you're finished, we should start working on the stalls. I have to leave in a little while to see about a horse. By the way, Cheryl, please call me Carlotta. After all, everyone here does. It makes me feel younger than I am."

Cheryl grinned happily and then the kids hurried to take their horses to the paddock, where the animals began to graze upon the wonderfully fresh grass.

*

"Wow, and it's really true that you panic as soon as you even think about riding or horses?" asked Sasha, as she slurped her banana milkshake.

Cathy nodded. "Well, yeah, but today I actually managed to look at a picture of a horse without panicking," she answered proudly.

"That's great! I think you'll get over everything. Say, just hypothetically, when you're ready, won't you try to get Rashid back? I mean, you have first dibs on riding him, don't you? You were there before Cheryl, weren't you?"

"Yes, but at the moment I just can't think about it, but . . . oh, I don't know." Cathy fooled around with the zipper on her sweatshirt.

Sasha looked at her over the rim of her glass. "You're not going to let someone mess up everything, are you?"

"Everything's already messed up," Cathy replied tearfully, and secretly she thought of her friends at the stable.

"I wouldn't let them do that to me! Show them who you are! Show them that you don't need them, and then . . . then get Rashid back!"

"I don't know if I even want to. When Carlotta decides to do something, then that's the way it stays. And now she's decided on Cheryl." Cathy was surprised to find out that she was closer to tears of disappointment than she was to tears of anger.

"Cheryl! Cheryl!" Sasha snorted disgustedly. "She just acts like she knows about horses, but she doesn't have a clue! You'll see, that woman — what was her name again? — she'll find that out pretty quickly, and she'll be glad when you can take over with Rashid again!"

Cathy looked at her pensively. "Do you think so?"

"Of course!" Sasha nodded encouragingly, and Cathy had the feeling that she'd never had a better friend than her new one.

"So, what about it? Will you try?" urged Sasha, and after a few seconds, which seemed like an eternity, Cathy began to nod slowly.

"Yeah, I think I'm going to try," she said almost too softly to be heard, and she suddenly sensed an enormous strength flowing into her.

Sasha grinned with satisfaction. "All right. Hey, I have to go now. If you'd like, we can get together again soon. It was great talking with you," she said, and motioned to the waiter to bring the bill.

"Oh, it's a shame that you have to leave already, but I'd like to get together again soon. You . . . you're really nice."

"You are too. And I can always find time for you! Well, almost always, but that's what friends do, isn't it?" The two girls got up, and Sasha gave Cathy a hug good-bye.

"So, take care, we'll get together soon," she said with a bright smile, before the two of them separated to go home.

"Thanks for your help," Cathy said quietly, waving to her new friend.

Sasha was very pleased with herself. *Wonderful,* she thought. *That went exactly according to plan! Cheryl, watch out, you're going to have some problems! No one calls me a liar and gets away with it!*

*

After Carlotta explained to Ricki and the other kids what she wanted them to do, she left to follow up on the phone call she received, regarding a man who was threatening to put down his horse if she didn't come and take it to her ranch immediately.

"I'm going to tell him in no uncertain terms what I think of him!" she mumbled to herself, upset, as she drove down the road. Carlotta was astonished, however, when, a little while later, she found herself in front of a large, luxurious house. Directly beside the house was a fabulous shed for horses, with a neighboring paddock on which a beautiful Black Forest mare was frolicking.

Somewhat confused, Carlotta looked again at the slip of paper on which she had written down the address. She kept staring at the house number and shaking her head.

64

I must have gotten something wrong, she thought. *This can't be the right address.*

"Hello! May I help you?"

Carlotta was startled. She hadn't noticed that a tall man in a green jogging suit had walked over to her car and was now looking at her a little condescendingly.

"Hello," she answered pleasantly. "I think I've made a mistake. Do you know a family named Travers, who are thinking about having a horse put down?"

The man raised one eyebrow and straightened up. "Are you from the animal shelter?"

Carlotta shook her head. "No. I'm Carlotta Mancini, and I —"

"Oh! The lady with the ranch for retired horses! Well, you're exactly as I imagined you. That was fast! Your reputation precedes you, Mrs. Mancini," he said, smiling slyly.

"What? What kind of reputation?" Warily, Carlotta looked into the man's eyes as she got out of her car awkwardly, with the help of her crutch.

"Well, they say that you come immediately when there's a horse that needs saving, especially one being put down. Apparently you've done this a few times before."

All of Carlotta's alarm bells were going off. "It seems that this is the right address, Mr. Travers. You *are* Mr. Travers, aren't you?" she asked, and all at once her friendliness disappeared. "By the way, you're not completely correct about my reputation."

"And why is that?"

"Because I also have the reputation of losing my temper when someone tries to get rid of a horse just because he's

65

tired of it or has a new toy!" she said angrily, staring at the man with hard eyes.

"According to the law, animals are property." Victor Travers dismissed Carlotta's words. "We human beings are free to change our minds at any time about what we like and what we don't like, what we want and don't want! If I wear a gray suit today, I can take a blue one out of the closet tomorrow just because I feel like it, if you catch my drift."

Carlotta thought she must have heard wrong. She had to force herself to stay calm.

"You mean that you see no difference between living creatures and your suits?" she asked through tightly clenched teeth.

Travers shrugged indifferently. *Why should I?* was his implied answer. "If I don't like my suit anymore, I can just throw it away."

"Uh-huh, and if your horse doesn't please you anymore, then you can just have it killed?" Carlotta couldn't believe this man.

"Yes, you could say that. Although a suit is at least a useful item, and a horse just costs time and money, without being all that useful."

"That is the limit!" Carlotta exploded and pointed her crutch at the man. "Why did you buy the horse in the first place? For prestige?"

Travers laughed. "Do you think I need that? No, a year ago my daughter thought she couldn't live without a horse. Now that she's older she's realized that a convertible is more interesting, and I have to admit, I agree with her."

"And there is no choice other than having the animal put down? Have you tried to sell it?"

"You don't think I'm going to take the time to squabble with someone. No, I just check this off my list and not have to think about it anymore. Ever!"

"Ever!" Carlotta nodded furiously. "I see."

Travers was getting impatient. "I don't know why I bothered to tell you all this. After all, it's none of your business what I do or don't do with my things. Anyway, why are you so upset? Didn't I call the animal shelter? I gave the horse a chance, right?" He grinned patronizingly at Carlotta, who was having trouble containing her anger toward this horrible man.

"A real chance? You know how little space there is at the animal shelter, especially for large animals. And you probably want the animal shelter to pay you for being allowed to pick up your mare, am I right?"

"Of course. And anyway, the animal is in good health and you have enough space, don't you?"

"I'm sure you understand that the animal shelters are struggling to survive. They need every dollar. How can you expect to get money when you offer an animal shelter your horse?"

"Then why don't you buy the mare? You're a Good Samaritan!"

"Good Samaritans don't have money growing on trees, either!"

Travers looked at the exasperated Carlotta scornfully. "If that's the way it is, then I wish you good day, my dear. It was nice to meet you," he said, and turned to go.

Such a jerk! thought Carlotta, struggling with her feelings. *He would actually put that beautiful animal down! Heavens, what kind of a world do we live in?*

"Oh, excuse me, I have one more question." Carlotta's forceful voice held Victor Travers back.

"What now? I'm pretty sure we've discussed everything. You don't want to pay, neither does the animal shelter, and so the animal will be put down."

"What do you do for a living, Mr. Travers? Somehow you seem familiar to me." Carlotta wanted to know.

"What? Why do you want to know?" Puzzled, the man added, "I work for the government."

Carlotta put on a friendly smile. "Oh, maybe the government would be interested in knowing how you feel about animals. Or even better, maybe our local paper will write a nice article about you. I bet people would love reading that. I know a good journalist who —"

"This is blackmail, Mrs. Mancini! Do you know the penalty for that?" Travers had turned pale. If there was anything he couldn't deal with, it was negative headlines in the press.

"I'm not blackmailing anyone, Mr. Travers. I just wanted to explain to you that I know a reporter who would love to write an article about a government official who supports the animal shelters financially. How much money did you want for this mare?"

Victor Travers balled his hands into angry fists. This woman had actually managed to outmaneuver him. If a nosy reporter started sniffing around, especially one who was trying to expose something negative about him, then his career would be over.

Furious, the man ground his teeth together, wishing he could chase Carlotta off his property, but he forced himself to smile instead.

"My dear Mrs. Mancini, I think you have an excellent idea. Oh, what I wanted to ask you is, would it be possible for you to keep my mare at your ranch? If you could take her, I would be truly grateful to you. And maybe I could somehow repay you for your kindness."

Carlotta began to grin broadly. "Well, look at that! It is possible to talk reasonably with you, Mr. Travers! Well, here's my suggestion: I will take your horse off your hands, and you will pay for its keep for one year, unless I find a good home for the mare before the year is up, in which case you would be freed from your monthly payment. It would be great if you would then pay the rest of the annual amount to the local animal shelter. Is that acceptable to you?"

Travers closed his eyes angrily. *This can't be happening!* he thought, inwardly shaking. *This woman is sharper than anyone I've ever met!*

"Okay, Mrs. Mancini, you win! I don't like to admit it, but you would be perfect for —"

"Thank you," Carlotta said, dismissing his gesture, "but I already have a job."

"Now, about that reporter," began Travers, but Carlotta looked at him innocently.

"What reporter? I don't know any reporter, if the payment is made by next week for — What's the horse's name, by the way?"

"Sheila. That beast, ah, that animal's name is Sheila. When will you be picking her up?" Travers's face was bright red.

"Oh, Sheila! A pretty name for a pretty horse!" Carlotta turned to go. "I'm sure it won't be a problem for you to bring the horse to me. In fact, I'm sure that you will be glad to do it! Please bring her to my ranch tomorrow. You probably already know where it's located. Would two o'clock *suit* you?"

Travers's breath was labored with rage. No one had ever gotten the best of Victor Travers, but he knew that Carlotta had won.

"Two o'clock! But only if you go away and I never have to see you again!"

"Fine by me. Thanks again. By the way, I feel the same way. I don't care if I never see you again! Unless, of course, you have another horse that you want to get rid of," grinned Carlotta, and then she got into her car.

"I've had enough of horses to last me a lifetime," snarled Travers. "I should have had the animal put down immediately!"

"But that would have damaged your image, wouldn't it, my dear Mr. Travers? Have a nice day. And don't forget, tomorrow at two o'clock," called Carlotta, happily. She started her car and drove slowly past the paddock.

"See you tomorrow, little Sheila. Be glad you're getting away from this place. I bet you didn't even know how much danger you were in," she murmured softly with an affectionate look at the mare, and then she hurried home.

Chapter 5

"When I see improvements like these, I wonder why we still use straw in the stalls," said Ricki, as she looked with fascination into Carlotta's stalls. "These mats seem ideal, and the special material Carlotta throws on top works well, too!"

"Well, the function of these mats is clear to me. The horse urine runs through and the mats keep the stalls more or less dry," commented Kevin. "But why do you need this stuff to scatter over it? Wouldn't plain sawdust do just as well? That special material is probably expensive."

"Sawdust isn't nearly as absorbent as this stuff," Lillian explained knowledgeably. "When used with the drain mats, you can be sure the horses are standing in dry stalls. I've seen this stuff at my father's friend's farm. It's really great!" Lillian grabbed a new bale of the material and pulled it into the next stall, where she distributed it evenly.

"And there's another advantage," she added. "The special material absorbs the wetness from the horse manure, so white horses stay white a lot longer than when you use straw— which would be perfect for Holli!"

"If it's that good, maybe we should talk to Jake about it."
Ricki grabbed a bale too.

Kevin laughed. "Maybe it would be better to talk to
our parents and Carlotta about it, since they would have to
pay for the mats and the special material. I'm not sure my
mother would be pleased to hear that this stuff is a lot more
expensive than straw."

"But you only have to buy the mats once, and — Hey,
Carlotta's back. I can't wait to hear about the horse she went
to see," called Cheryl, with a glance out the window. "I
wonder what that was all about."

"Me too!" her new friends said in unison, and they ran
outside to greet Carlotta.

"Well, gang, how far did you get?"

"Everything's ready," reported Lillian briskly.

"Great! You must really have worked hard!" Carlotta
was obviously pleased with what they had accomplished,
and she patted each of them on the shoulder, before she
turned to Lillian.

"Lillian, would it be possible for your father to bring
Jonah over tomorrow, about noon?" she asked.

Lillian was shocked. "What? Tomorrow? So soon? I
won't be able to really say good-bye to him."

"Oh, come on, Lillian. You've been saying good-bye for
at least three months," Ricki said, grinning.

"That's true. Still, it's awfully quick."

"Lillian, if I know you at all, you'll probably ride over
here every day. Jonah isn't in another world, after all, and
I need a stall companion for Sheila," said Carlotta as she
winked.

"What?"

"Who's Sheila?"

"You went to look at a horse for the ranch?"

"And you didn't tell us anything? That's mean."

The friends beamed and Carlotta nodded, smiling.

"It's a Black Forest mare, and from the look of her, she's not very old, and she's in great shape!" she told them.

"But then she's not really a horse for the ranch," said Ricki.

"Yes she is, in a way, because she would have been put down if I hadn't taken her. But I'll tell you all about it while we have something to drink. I need a cup of coffee!"

*

"I love Black Forest horses!" enthused Cheryl, who was riding beside Ricki. "You don't see them very often because they're new to the U.S. They're not particularly big, but they're strong, and their super-long light-colored manes just fascinate me. Black Forest horses were used more for pulling wagons and carriages, but they're so gentle and good-natured they've become popular family riding horses. They —"

"Thanks, Cheryl, but we know what Black Forest horses look like and what they're used for," laughed Kevin.

"Sorry, they really are my favorite horse breed."

"Oh, Rashid, did you hear that? You're going to have some competition!" Ricki glanced at the dun horse, pretending to look sad.

"Oh, stop it!" Cheryl bent over Rashid's neck and buried her face in his mane. "You have no competition. Don't let them worry you," she whispered to him.

"Yeah, yeah! Until you see Sheila, and then he's history," teased Lillian. "Say, what do you think Carlotta's going to do when all of her stalls are full, and then she discovers another horse that needs to be saved?"

"It could be a real problem," said Kevin. "But after all, she can't save all the horses in the world, and when these stalls are full, she won't have any money left over, either."

"Didn't she say that she wants to try and find homes for some of the animals? I mean, if someone is just looking for a companion horse, they could take an older animal without any problem, couldn't they?" Ricki stroked Diablo across the ridge of his mane. "And horses like Sheila, for example, could even be sold as riding or workhorses."

Cheryl made a face. "Oh, that would really be a shame," she said, disappointed.

"Cheryl, think about it. If Carlotta could find a good home for Sheila, then she'd have a vacant stall for a really neglected or abused creature. After all, Carlotta isn't running a riding ranch; she wants her ranch to be a place where aging, ailing or abused horses will be looked after and cared for," exclaimed Kevin.

"Yeah," Cheryl answered. "I know, but do you have to talk about Sheila being sold before she's even in the stable?"

"Wow, you don't even know her yet and you're already upset."

"I like Black Forest horses, a *lot*," repeated Cheryl, with emphasis.

"Hey, people, how about a short gallop before our new friend here has a complete breakdown," Lillian said, shortening Holli's reins.

74

"Yeah! That'll put her in a different frame of mind. Come on, Rashid, show us what you can do," shouted Ricki, and once she was sure that Kevin and Cheryl were prepared for the change of pace, she pressed her calves against Diablo's belly and let him go into a gallop.

As always, when she heard the thunder of her horse's hooves on the ground, Ricki's heart seemed to adapt itself completely to the rhythm, and there was nothing around her more important at that moment than her connection with Diablo, her dream horse.

The trees flew by, as indistinct as ghosts disappearing into thin air.

I love this horse so much, thought Ricki, and she felt an unending gratitude in her heart. But unlike her usual happy reveries, this time she was distracted.

She stole a quick glance to the side, where Rashid was galloping with his new rider, neck and neck with Diablo, and she realized that she was startled by the fact that it wasn't Cathy in that saddle.

"Awesome!" Cheryl called out just then, overjoyed, and Ricki forced herself to smile.

Darn it, as nice as Cheryl is, I miss Cathy! thought Ricki, and there was nothing she would have liked more at that moment than to have her friend riding at her side. She sighed loudly and tried to get her mind back to reality. After all, there was no sense in hanging onto the past. What had happened had happened, and nothing could change that.

*

Cathy sat in her room looking at her unopened photo album, which she had dug out from the bottom drawer of her dresser. She knew that there were more pictures of Rashid than of her, but after the conversation with Sasha she had decided to fight her fear. Yes, she was going to get rid of this phobia once and for all! But now, ten minutes later, she was sitting timidly at her desk with her hands folded on top of the album and she couldn't seem to open it.

You're not going to let Cheryl take Rashid away from you, are you? Sasha's words still hammered in her head. *She ruined everything! She knows nothing about horses! You're not going to let —!*

Cathy closed her eyes for a moment and took several slow, deep breaths.

"I'm going to look at these photos, even if it makes me crazy!" she said to herself quietly, and tried to make her voice sound determined and strong. With her hands trembling, she opened the album.

After a few family photos, she saw a portrait of Rashid, in which he was looking directly at her, and her heart skipped a beat. She covered her eyes with her hands, to keep from seeing the proud look in the horse's eyes, but in her mind's eye he just kept staring right at her.

Cathy reminded herself that this had always been her favorite photo, but nevertheless, at the moment, it was impossible for her to bear looking at him. Upset, she turned away, leaving the album lying still open on the table.

You're not going to let Cheryl take Rashid away from you . . . you're not going to let —

"No!" Cathy screamed suddenly. "No, I don't want that to

happen! But how in the world am I ever going to win Rashid back if I can't even bear to look at a photo of him?"

You're never going to make it! her inner voice told her, making her feel almost desperate, but then she straightened up and forced herself to turn around.

"I'm stronger than you are, you stupid fear!" she said out loud. "I am going to look at Rashid's photo, and it's not going to bother me at all!"

The girl tried to stop thinking entirely, while her eyes slowly moved to the picture lying in front of her.

She focused on the top corner of the photo and let her eyes rest there for a few minutes. Then, when she sensed that her heartbeat had slowed down to almost normal, she allowed her eyes to move down an inch, forcing herself to look at Rashid's ears, which were pointed attentively.

Cathy remembered how she had clicked her tongue over and over, until Rashid had positioned his ears like that. That made her smile. Clicking her tongue so much had made her cough loudly, which had spooked Rashid and made him run away right after she had taken his picture.

She saw the dun horse in her mind, as he had been on that day, and immediately her fear returned. She quickly closed the album and tried to calm herself by breathing slowly and regularly.

Then she went to the window and stared off into the distance, her eyes unfocused. She was proud of herself, that she had at least dared to start healing, but it was clear to her now how much she still had to accomplish before she could look at Rashid, or any other horse, without fear.

"But I'll do it!" she encouraged herself, nodding

emphatically. "And someday . . . someday I'm going to ride again!" Sighing, she placed her hot forehead against the cool windowpane.

*

"What do you want?" Cheryl's voice turned icy when she recognized Sasha's voice on the other end of the line.

"Oh, come on, Cheryl, please don't stay mad at me! I'm really sorry about what I said," simpered Sasha.

Although Cheryl knew that Sasha wasn't being sincere, she couldn't be mean and just hang up on her, so she waited, silently, to hear what Sasha had to say.

"Can't we still be friends?" asked Sasha, in a pleading tone.

"I don't know."

"Hey, I'll tell you a secret. I had a talk with Cathy today, totally unexpectedly. You know her. She used to ride Rashid. And guess what? She's planning on going to Ricki's stable and booting you out of there! Isn't that unbelievable?" Sasha paused a little before continuing. "I thought you should know."

"And you're not lying again, are you?" asked Cheryl softly.

"No! Honestly!"

"Okay! Thank you, Sasha, for telling me."

"See, I'm not as bad as you thought. Want to get together again?"

"Ah, no, not today. I still have some homework to do," Cheryl lied, crossing her fingers.

"Okay, then I'll see you tomorrow at school," Sasha replied, and then hung up immediately.

"Bye!" answered Cheryl, but all she heard was the buzz of a disconnected line.

If what Sasha had just told her were really true, then there would probably be trouble at the stable for a while. She wasn't willing to give up Rashid after such a short time. On the other hand, if she were Cathy, she would probably try to get Rashid back again too.

"Darn!" she said to herself and went to her room. She had some things to think over.

*

Lillian's father brought old Jonah to Carlotta's ranch the next day, just before noon. Carlotta could see that it wasn't easy for him to say good-bye to the big horse.

"I'll miss him," said Dave Bates, happy and sad at the same time. He patted Jonah firmly on the neck and gave him a huge carrot.

Carlotta smiled. "Thanks again for letting me keep him so long at your place until everything was ready here."

"Don't mention it." Lillian's father said, waving her words away. He hurried back to his car. After all, Carlotta didn't need to see that he was having a hard time holding back a few tears.

Jonah was standing all by himself in his new roomy stall, looking all around curiously. *Everything looks great here,* he seemed to be saying. *Large stall, good hay, but pretty boring if I have to be here all alone.*

Carlotta rubbed the horse's soft muzzle and spoke to him in a friendly tone.

"Don't worry, you big bear, you'll have company in about two hours, if that fine gentleman hasn't forgotten our appointment. You'll see, I've found a really attractive lady companion for you. You're going to love her!"

Jonah pointed his ears, looking as though he had understood every word she said.

"So, my good boy, you have a rack full of hay, and if it's all right with you, I'm going to go get something to eat to build up my strength for the meeting with Mr. Travers. Don't worry, I'm definitely coming back!" added Carlotta, laughing when Jonah whinnied after her accusingly. Just two minutes later, however, the animal had turned to his feed and was chewing contentedly on the tender stalks of hay.

*

Right on time, the horse trailer of Wolcott and Company drove up to the yard in front of Carlotta's ranch. Victor Travers had arranged for a company driver to transport Sheila to Carlotta's ranch. He didn't want any further dealings with that stubborn woman.

"Hi. Am I at the right place?" the driver asked her pleasantly when Carlotta came out of the house.

"If you've brought a Black Forest mare by the name of Sheila, you are!" laughed Carlotta.

The driver let the huge hydraulic loading flap down. "You'll have to sign this," he said, and handed Carlotta two sheets of paper and a pen. Then he went into the transporter and came out again with Sheila.

"Is this the horse?" he asked, to make sure, and Carlotta nodded happily when she saw the mare.

"Yes, that's Sheila. Isn't she beautiful?"

The driver grinned. "Well, I'm a big fan of little Shetland ponies myself, but to each his own, right? Where do you want me to put her?"

Carlotta indicated that he should follow her, and she hobbled forward on one crutch.

"What a great stable! You don't see one like this every day."

Carlotta couldn't help blushing a little with pride.

"Please, put her into the stall next to Jonah here."

The driver nodded, and after Sheila had been taken care of he hurried off.

"Thanks again," Carlotta called after him.

"Welcome home, you two!" said Carlotta, gazing affectionately at her first two stall guests. "May I offer you an opening day treat, courtesy of Mercy Ranch?"

Jonah stretched his head over the top of the stall to see what was happening, and then he took the treat very carefully from his owner's hand. Sheila, on the other hand, just observed Carlotta suspiciously from the side. She didn't seem at all interested in Jonah, and the treat didn't seem enough to make her take even one step toward Carlotta voluntarily.

"Well, what's wrong, little one?" Carlotta asked in a soothing voice. "You have to get used to us a little first, don't you? Take your time. We'll get used to each other. Don't worry, I'm sure you'll be happy here."

For a while, Carlotta just watched the mare, without getting any closer. But then she laid the treat on the top of her stall.

"If you want it, you can come and get it yourself," she said quietly. "You just have to be careful that it doesn't fall down! I'll let you two beauties alone now, so you can get acquainted with each other. 'Bye for now, you two, and enjoy your feed!"

Carlotta walked away slowly, and at the door to the stable she looked back and realized with a smile that both horses were observing her attentively.

*

When the last school period was over, Ricki stormed past Cathy, who had paid no attention to her the whole day, and met up with her other friends at the bike stand.

"I wonder if Sheila arrived yet?" Ricki was really excited when she realized that the first horses would now be in the stable at Mercy Ranch.

"Well, Jonah is definitely there. Dad took him over this morning," said Lillian.

"Let's ride over to Carlotta's right after we go home and change," suggested Kevin, but Ricki objected.

"Have you forgotten how much homework we have? The new substitute teacher seems to love giving pop quizzes and homework!"

"Do you still have Ms. Murphy for English?" Lillian said, groaning at the thought of her former teacher.

"Yeah, but she's been out sick, and it looks like we'll be stuck with Mr. Reid until the end of the year."

"Well, he's got to be better than 'The Murph.' By the way, how was Cathy's mood today?" Lillian wanted to know.

"Don't ask. If she keeps up the silent treatment, I think I'll ask to get my seat changed. I can't take it anymore. She just keeps ignoring me."

"Look over there. Apparently she's found a new friend." Kevin pointed over at the school entrance, where Cathy and

Sasha were standing and talking with each other, their arms gesticulating.

Cheryl, who was just coming out the school door, stopped for a moment, but as Sasha winked at her like a conspirator, she pretended that she didn't see the two of them and ran over to the others quickly.

"Hey, what's going on with those two? Could you hear what they were saying?" Kevin asked, curious.

"No!" answered Cheryl brusquely.

"Is something wrong? You're acting strange today, too!"

"Well, Sasha told me Cathy wants to ride Rashid again, and . . ." she began slowly.

"You don't believe that, do you?" Kevin interrupted. "Cathy freaks out when she just hears the word 'horse'!"

"I think Sasha told you another one of her lies," Lillian said, and Ricki and Kevin agreed.

"She said she's going to try to get more information out of Cathy, and that I should pretend that we don't have anything to do with one another, for the time being," Cheryl reported further.

"Oh! I thought you were finished with her anyway, or did I miss something?" Ricki was puzzled.

"Well, Sasha called me, said she was sorry, and asked me if I want to be friends with her again."

"And little Cheryl just gave that big liar a hug, didn't she?" responded Kevin.

Ricki looked at him accusingly. "I think that's between Sasha and Cheryl," she said slowly.

"Okay, but I'd be very careful with a friend who lies!"

"C'mon, people, that's enough drama for today. I'm

hungry and I want to go home now," Lillian interrupted. "When are we getting together? Same time as always?"

"Hmm, maybe half an hour later, otherwise I'll never get my homework done," said Ricki.

"Okay, I'll see you then, and we'll go straight to Carlotta's. I can't wait to see what's happening!" Grinning, Lillian, waved good-bye and then pedaled away.

"How come she's not waiting for us? We're going in the same direction she is," Kevin wondered.

"Silly! Didn't you notice she's going in the other direction? I think she wants to visit Josh before she rides home," Ricki said, laughing.

"Oh! Well, then, bye, Cheryl, see you later this afternoon!"

"Yup, see ya!" Cheryl watched her two friends ride away, then jumped on her bike and rode home. On the way, she thought about Sasha and Cathy, who had been laughing a little too loudly, she thought, as she came out the main door.

There's definitely something going on, thought Cheryl, but at the moment she didn't want to think about it. She tried instead to imagine what Carlotta's new horse, the Black Forest mare, looked like. She was excited about meeting Sheila, who was sure to be at the ranch by now.

Chapter 6

Cathy sat at the kitchen table with her mother and pushed food around on her plate listlessly. Her head was full of questions. Would she actually be able to overcome her fear, and if so, how could she convince Carlotta — and her mother — to let her ride Rashid again? She wondered how her old friends would react, but an even bigger problem was that she didn't know how she would ever get her mother's permission to get up in the saddle again.

Cathy sighed softly.

"Don't you feel well?" asked Mrs. Sutherland with a long look at her daughter. "You haven't eaten a bite, and I always thought you liked chicken nuggets!"

"I do," answered Cathy brusquely, and she leaned her head on one hand as she drew her fork through the mashed potatoes.

"Did something happen at school?" Cathy's mother questioned her further.

"No. Everything's fine."

"Then are you still mad that I told your friends never to come back here again?"

"No! Definitely not!" Cathy snorted scornfully. *Friends!*
Some friends they turned out to be! I can do just fine without
them! But what if I want to ride Rashid again? Then I'd
be forced to get along with them. She took a deep breath,
gathered up all her courage, and finally said, "Mom, I . . . I
want . . . I want to ride again someday!"

Mrs. Sutherland, who had just gotten up to put her plate
in the sink, turned around quickly and stared at her daughter
in disbelief.

"You're not serious, are you? How can you think that I
would ever allow you even to go into a stable — much less
ride again — after all that's happened?"

Cathy frowned, and didn't look at her mother. She had
expected that answer.

"You could have died in that fall, Cathy! Haven't you
realized that yet? Horses are dangerous!"

"They aren't any more dangerous than other animals!"
countered the girl. "And I could have died from that
ruptured appendix . . . probably even more easily than from
the fall!"

Mrs. Sutherland knew that her daughter was right, but
she didn't want her to win the argument.

"Cathy, you're afraid of horses! You can't even look
at a photo of one without bursting into tears, and you're
dreaming of getting back on a horse? Who told you that you
have to ride again? Was it your friend Ricki? I think I'm
going to have to have another serious talk with her! I —"

Cathy shook her head. "No! It wasn't my friend Ricki!
It's my —"

"Oh, come on! Don't lie to me!" Mrs. Sutherland's eyes

86

began to sparkle with anger. "Just forget this nonsense, for once and for all!"

"But —"

"Stop it. I don't want to hear another word!"

Cathy pushed back her plate in disgust and stood up, glancing once more at her mother sadly. She passed her silently and was about to go to her room, but as she left the kitchen she stopped abruptly. Suddenly she had an idea how she might be able to convince her mother that her riding accident wasn't really connected directly with Rashid being spooked.

"That's it! At least it's worth a try," Cathy murmured to herself, and instead of going back to her room, she left the house, got on her bike, and rode off.

*

"Hey, what are you doing later today? Will you be riding or do you want to get together?" Sasha had called Cheryl on her cell phone.

"Well, we're going to ride over to Carlotta's, that's Mrs. Mancini. I'm sorry, I won't have time," Cheryl was holding her cell phone between her ear and her shoulder as she was changing into her riding clothes.

"What are you going to do at her place?"

"She has two horses at her ranch now, and we want to take a look at them," Cheryl volunteered.

"Oh. Well, then, have fun," Sasha said. She was about to hang up, but then she changed her mind. "Cheryl? Are you still there? When will you be back?"

"I have no idea. We'll probably leave about four o'clock, and I doubt we'll be back before seven. Why do you ask?"

"No reason. I thought maybe we could get together afterward, but that's going to be too late for me. Maybe tomorrow. Bye!"

"Yeah, maybe. See ya." Cheryl put her cell phone down and turned her head back and forth a little to free the tension in her neck.

"I need to get a phone with a speaker," she mumbled to herself as she slid into her riding boots and started off toward the Sulais' stable.

*

"There you are, finally," called Ricki from a distance, as Lillian came hurrying into the barn. "We've been waiting for you forever!"

"You always exaggerate," panted her friend as she rushed over to Holli. "Why do mothers always have to come up with something they want us to do at the very worst time? Can't they tell when we have other plans?"

Kevin grinned. "I think that's the inevitable responsibility of youth."

"And where'd you get that idea?"

"Where do you think? From my mother, of course."

"Hey, you two already brushed Holli! Thanks!" Lillian smiled and hurried to saddle her horse. "Being stressed out when you're saddling your horse is awful," she complained. "And it makes the horse nervous."

"Lillian, stress is your middle name," teased Ricki, and winked happily over to Cheryl, who was already leading Rashid out of his stall.

"Ha, ha, ha! I'm finished! It's just too bad that I always

have to wait for you guys," laughed Holli's owner as she slipped the halter over his head and grabbed the reins.

"Great, we can get going. I can't tell you how anxious I am to see Sheila!" Cheryl's eyes began to glow.

"We'll have to make sure that Rashid is in his stall tonight, and not Sheila. We don't dare let Cheryl out of our sight at Carlotta's, either," joked Kevin as he mounted.

"Oh, so you think I could do that, huh?"

"Of course! The way you've been raving about that mare, even though you've never seen her, I bet you're capable of smuggling her to this stable."

"Nobody would notice it here, would they?" Cheryl grinned right back at them. "Oh, can someone hold Rashid for a minute? I left my cell phone in the stall."

"Sure." Kevin reached for Rashid's reins and Cheryl ran back into the stall.

Several minutes passed, and Cheryl still hadn't returned.

"What's she doing?" asked Lillian impatiently.

"Sorry, people, I had to look for it!" called Cheryl, and she ran back and grabbed her reins.

"C'mon, hurry up. We're already late. We can talk while we ride."

"Calm down, Ricki. After all, we didn't tell Carlotta we'd be there at a specific time."

"Yeah, but I can hardly wait to see the new horse," admitted Ricki, and she was glad that they were finally under way.

*

" . . . and even if I manage to get rid of my fear, my mother will never let me ride again," said Cathy, her voice choked by tears. Her hand, which was holding the cell phone, began to shake. She had been back for about an hour, and although, just a few moments before, she had been convinced that she would ride again someday, now she was completely depressed. Her hopes had been dashed when she tried to look at Rashid's photo again, for a little longer this time, and thinking about the earlier conversation with her mother was the last straw.

"Oh, come on," comforted Sasha. "I'm sure that when your mom sees that you're so much better, she'll be more ready to talk about it!"

Cathy sniffed. "Do you really think so? I don't!"

On the other end of the line, Sasha rolled her eyes. *This constant whining is really getting on my nerves!* she thought, but she didn't let Cathy know how she felt.

"You shouldn't be so negative! Hey, have you looked at the photo album yet today?"

Cathy nodded silently, not thinking that Sasha couldn't see her.

"If you haven't, then do it today. You know you have to get used to looking at Rashid if you ever want to ride him again. Oh, yeah, I just thought of something else," Sasha said, pausing dramatically. "I've been thinking about you, and I'm convinced that you have to go back to the stable in order to get over your trauma!"

Cathy was startled. "*In* the stable? How's that going to work? Do you think I can just go up to Ricki and my buddies and say, 'Hi, you guys, here I am again,' and act as though nothing happened? No, Sasha, I don't think I can do that!"

"Do you want to ride Rashid again or not?"

90

"I do, but —"

"Then you have to go to the stable again! Honestly, I'm thinking more about the stable than about your fair-weather friends. After all, you just have to get used to the atmosphere at the stable again. Smell the horses, and just look at the animals, so that your inner self mends."

"Hmm," said Cathy pensively. "Maybe you're right, but . . . the others —?"

"The others, the others. Don't let them get to you. At the moment they're totally unimportant."

"But they're always at the stable. I won't be able to avoid them!"

Sasha grinned. "Not always! For example, this afternoon they're all riding over to visit the lady who runs Mercy Ranch."

Cathy hesitated. "How do you know that?" she asked.

"How do you think? Cheryl would do anything to get back in with me."

"Okay, but what's that supposed to mean, that there won't be anyone in the stable this afternoon?"

"Cheryl, you are really slow! I thought maybe we could meet up now and go over there together. Then you can get used to the stable again without having the others around. Maybe you can even manage to stroke that stupid donkey or that ugly pony. They're really not scary. At least that would be a beginning, wouldn't it?"

Just thinking about touching Chico or Salina almost turned Cathy's stomach with fear. On the other hand, if she could make herself touch the two of them, the road to Rashid wouldn't be quite as long. Then she registered what Sasha had just said about the animals, and got angry.

"Chico isn't stupid and Salina isn't ugly! Why do you say that? And anyway, why would you want to come with me?"

Sasha laughed a little too loudly. "Well, it's simple. I just wanted to test you. As long as you try to defend them, you can't be that afraid of them," she explained hastily.

"That's true," Cathy said, joining in the laughter of her new friend.

"Good, so we're going?" Sasha wanted to know.

Cathy took a deep breath, with her eyes closed. "Okay," she answered after a few seconds. "I'll do it. I think you're right. I don't have any idea if I can do this, or what I'll say to Ricki's parents or Jake if they turn up, but I'll think of something."

"Then I'll see you soon. I think I can be at your house in about ten minutes," responded Sasha, and ended the conversation before Cathy could change her mind. A crafty smile stole across Sasha's face, and she rubbed her hands in anticipation. "If you only knew," Sasha murmured to herself with smug satisfaction, and then she rushed out of her room to get to Cathy's house on time.

*

The friends had loosened their girths, put more comfortable halters on the horses, and tied them to the heavy metal rings attached to the hitching rails outside Carlotta's stable. Then they all went into the stable together, laughing and chatting.

"Hey, Carlotta!" Kevin called, right inside the door to the stalls, and the owner of the ranch looked at him accusingly.

"Oops, sorry!" the boy apologized immediately when he realized what his loud voice had caused.

The kids stood stock-still.

Carlotta was standing in the half-opened door to Sheila's stall. She had held out her arms and was trying to get the timid animal to come to her. When Kevin's voice boomed, Sheila's ears jerked back and lay flat on her head, and she showed the whites of her eyes, emanating fear. If Carlotta had even a ghost of a chance a few minutes ago of getting a little bit closer to Sheila, that chance was completely gone now. Sheila's look went from hate to fear, and she retreated into the farthest corner of her stall.

Sighing, Carlotta decided to retreat for the time being, and to try to win the horse's trust a little later.

"Oh, no, I'm really, really sorry," mumbled Kevin, embarrassed. "I had no idea —"

"Didn't anyone ever tell you kids that a stable has to be calm? You all have your own horses and you know you can't shout when you're around them. Especially not when you go into someone else's stable and there could be skittish animals!" Carlotta spoke quietly but seriously.

Kevin nodded, looking guilty. He was worried about losing Carlotta's good will, but she gestured to him, showing that all was forgiven.

"Come on over here. After all, you're here to welcome the new arrivals, right?"

The friends came forward, slowly and silently, and stopped about six feet from Sheila.

"Wow, she's beautiful!" Cheryl whistled softly in admiration, as she stared at the Black Forest mare.

Jonah, greedy for some attention, stretched his muscular neck way over the top of the stall and greeted Lillian with a contented whinny.

The girl approached him slowly and then took his huge head in her arms.

"Well, old boy, how do you like it here?" she asked him softly as she laid her cheek on the horse's wide brow. "I'll miss you, but I promise that I'll visit a lot!" Lillian swallowed a few times, but then she managed to smile. "This is the best place in the world for horses," she admitted, and pushed a carrot between Jonah's lips.

The old horse chewed the treat contentedly, as he searched for more with his nose on Lillian's shirt.

Lillian laughed softly and pushed Jonah's head aside before he could drool carrot saliva all over her clothes.

Sheila's ears had perked forward at the sound of her stall mate's chewing, and now the pretty animal was peering over at him, unsure of what to do.

"She is really adorable," commented Ricki. She couldn't stop looking at the mare. "What a shame that she's so shy and scared."

Kevin nodded. "What in the world did her former owner do to her?" he asked.

Carlotta shrugged her shoulders. "I have no idea, and I doubt we'll ever find out. It will probably take a while for her to trust people again, and we'll have to be careful until then. Frightened horses are unpredictable, because they're always on the defensive. So, be careful for the next few weeks, and pay attention. Don't get too close to her stall. With an animal like this, it's possible that she'll bite or kick if she feels threatened."

"Poor Sheila," whispered Cheryl, full of compassion. She felt a huge wave of sympathy for the horse. She's the horse I've always dreamed of, thought the girl, sighing silently.

She couldn't help feeling a little envious of Carlotta. This wonderful animal belonged to her, and not just Sheila, but also the wonderful Rashid, Jonah, and even little Salina. When the girl looked around the huge stable, with its many empty stalls waiting for horses that would need a caring home, she wished that she were Carlotta and that this was her stable, and these her horses.

"What are you thinking about?" asked Ricki and she poked Cheryl, gently. "Okay, I admit it, that was a stupid question," she said, grinning. "It's so completely obvious that you've fallen in love with Sheila. Anyone could see that from a hundred feet away."

"Come on, kids. Who's up for some apple cider and donuts?" Carlotta put a hand on Ricki's shoulder and leaned on her crutch with the other hand.

"Oh, that sounds great," Lillian replied, and she tore herself away from Jonah.

"Good, then let's go." Carlotta and the others walked down the corridor slowly, although Cheryl stayed motionless in front of Sheila's stall.

"Aren't you coming?" called Carlotta, when she noticed that the girl had stayed put.

Sighing, Cheryl turned aside and followed the others, who were waiting for her at the door.

"Oh, please, Carlotta, I'm not thirsty. Couldn't I stay for a few more minutes . . . I mean . . . Sheila . . . she's . . . " she stammered.

The ranch owner smiled, understanding immediately. In her younger days, she had been more interested in horses than in people.

"Okay," she said. "But please be careful and promise me that you'll keep your distance. I don't want anything to happen."

Cheryl nodded, beaming. "Thank you! It'll be fine, really. I'll be there in just a few minutes," she promised, and ran back to Sheila quickly.

"Yeah, yeah!" grinned Carlotta. "I know very well what you kids mean by 'a few minutes'! Hey, Kevin, would you please take a little hay outside with you and give it to your horses? We don't want them going hungry while we feast, do we?"

*

Cathy and Sasha weren't far from the Sulais' stable when Cathy began to groan and clutch her hand to her stomach.

"What's wrong?" Sasha looked at her questioningly, and slowed her bike down a bit.

"I feel sick," admitted Cathy. "I feel like I'm going to throw up, if you want to know the truth!"

Sasha grinned. "You're not going to give up now, are you?"

"I . . . I don't know. Honestly, right now, I just want to turn around and go back home."

Sasha's expression hardened. *You idiot!* she thought, looking at Cathy. *Don't mess this up for me!*

"Oh, come on, don't be a chicken. You'll make it. Just imagine the look on the others' faces when you walk right into the stable and wrap your arms around Rashid as if nothing happened!"

"Yeah, I know, you're right, but —"

"But, but, but . . . you're always saying that! I keep talking and talking and trying to find the best therapy for you and you keep saying 'but'! It's starting to get on my nerves!"

Cathy stared straight ahead, feeling guilty. "I'm sorry, Sasha," she said quietly. "I know you're doing everything you can to help me, and I really am grateful to you, but —"

"Again with the 'but'! Look, let me spell it out for you, Catherine Sutherland, are we going to keep going so you can confront a little pony and an even tinier donkey, or should we turn back? I'll tell you one thing, though. If you go home now, I'll never try to help you again. Is that clear?" Sasha made a face and pretended to be insulted, although inwardly, she was almost exploding with anger. Would this idiot actually manage to ruin her brilliant plan?

"So what's it going to be?" she asked.

Cathy took a deep breath and then nodded. "Okay. But you have to promise me that you won't tell the others if I don't manage to touch Chico or Salina."

Sasha turned a thankful face up to the sky, and then she turned to Cathy with her most winning smile. "Absolutely, I promise!" she replied seriously.

"Hey, why are you doing this for me?" asked Cathy.

"What do you mean?"

"Well, why do you want to come with me, to help me to overcome my fear, and stuff?"

That's what I'm asking myself, too, thought Sasha, but she said, "That's what friends are for. I'm sure you'd be there for me too, if I were in your situation."

Cathy nodded gratefully. *Strange, I would never have imagined Sasha could be this nice*, she thought, and pedaled faster. All of a sudden she had the feeling that with Sasha to help her, she could really get her fear under control.

Yeah, I'll make it! she thought, and was even feeling

relieved by the time they left the bikes in front of the stable entrance.

"Well? Are you ready to confront the hoofed monsters?" teased Sasha, on purpose this time.

"Yes!" Cathy's answer sounded sure and strong, even though the color of her face indicated something completely different.

"Then let's go!" Sasha took Cathy's arm and they entered the stable unnoticed.

*

Cheryl stood in front of Sheila's stall and waited until she could no longer hear the voices of her friends.

She took one more step closer, and avoided looking straight into the eyes of the mare.

"Hey, you," she spoke quietly and affectionately, which made Sheila curious. "Why are you so afraid of people? Did some idiot hurt you? Hit you? Kick you? Believe me, not everyone is bad, and there are lots of people who would do anything to give wonderful creatures like you a nice home. And Carlotta is one of them. Did you know that Carlotta brought you here so that you never have to suffer again? Yeah, Sheila, that's the truth. I bet you have no idea how lucky you are!"

The mare listened attentively to the girl's words. Even Jonah had turned toward her, but he soon realized that Cheryl was interested only in his neighbor. He retreated, a little insulted, and scraped his hoof on the dirt before deciding to lie down and take a little nap.

Cheryl, meanwhile, kept talking to Sheila in a calm, soothing voice, telling her all kinds of things.

98

"It was just lucky chance that I got to go to Ricki's place and ride Rashid. Do you know Rashid? He's a wonderful horse. But can I tell you something? I like you even better! Have I already told you that you're the most beautiful horse I have ever seen? I would give anything to make you mine!"

Carefully, Cheryl took a few steps toward the stall. She raised her hands slowly and put them on the top of the wall that separated her from Sheila.

Dreamily, the girl sighed. "You are really special, Sheila!" she whispered. Suddenly Cheryl had the feeling that her heart was going to stop beating as the animal stretched its neck out slowly in her direction, breathing in the scent of the human being who was speaking so gently to it.

"Come on, sweetie, I won't hurt you. I promise. Come on," urged Cheryl, reaching her hand out carefully.

Keep your distance! I don't want anything to happen! Carlotta's voice hammered in her head all of a sudden. Frightened at the thought, Cheryl almost took a few steps backward, but Sheila's ears, which were standing straight up, signaled to her that the animal wasn't feeling threatened by her. The girl stayed put, her heart beating wildly.

"If you want me to touch you, you'll have to come over here." Cheryl smiled at the mare, and her legs began to shake with excitement as Sheila moved a little closer to her.

"See? You can do it. Look what I have for you. Would you like a treat? I brought this just for you." She slowly and cautiously moved her arm back to get a piece of dried apple out of her jeans pocket, and offered it to the horse on the palm of her hand.

Cheryl sensed that the next few minutes would decide if she was going to win Sheila's trust.

I just hope no one comes into the stable, she thought. *I hope Carlotta doesn't decide to come looking for me. I said a few minutes, but it's probably been at least half an hour since the others left. Oh, please, don't anyone come in right now and ruin everything. I'm so close to getting Sheila to lose her fear and trust me.* Slowly, carefully, Cheryl began to open the sliding door while speaking softly to Sheila, Carlotta's warning completely forgotten.

Chapter 7

Cathy stood in the familiar stable corridor with Sasha and let her gaze wander. "Strange," she murmured. "I'm standing here, where I have stood so often, and I feel like a stranger."

"Oh, don't be silly. Things haven't changed that much since the last time you were here," commented Sasha.

"That's true, but you know what's missing? It's the feeling of friendship that I always felt when I came here."

Suddenly Cathy was startled. Chico and Salina, who were dozing in the last stall, had been awakened by the girls' voices and were now making themselves heard, as loudly as possible. The high whinny of the pony and the hee-haw of the donkey echoed through the corridor, and the two animals stretched their heads above the top of the stall curiously.

Cathy retreated, pale as a ghost, several yards away from the stall.

"Wait, Cathy, where are you going? The two of them aren't about to jump over the top of the stall, are they?" Sasha held on to Cathy's arm, adding to her new friend's panic.

"Let go of me!" Cathy screamed. She pulled herself free from Sasha's grip and stumbled outside, where she leaned against the stable wall and took deep breaths.

Sasha rubbed her hands together. *Wonderful,* she thought, *now I'm not being watched, at least for the moment.* She walked quickly over to Diablo's stall. Tied to the metal ring fastened to the wall was a rope, which in turn was attached to Diablo's cobalt-blue halter.

Sasha pulled a little bottle out of her jeans pocket, reached for the halter, and dribbled a few drops of a colorless liquid onto the noseband and the piece that went across his neck.

The girl kept looking around to make sure that no one saw what she was doing. After a few seconds, she walked toward the stable door and saw that Cathy was still standing in the same spot.

"Don't you want to try again?" asked Sasha, pretending to care, but Cathy just shook her head.

"Oh, too bad! Those two little ones are really cute! You don't mind if I go in again and pet them, do you?"

"No, go ahead," Cathy replied quietly. Sasha had a satisfied look on her face as she returned to the stalls.

Without hesitating, she reached for Holli's and then Sharazan's halters, and wet the two headpieces with the liquid she had brought with her. The only halter she left alone was the one belonging to Rashid. Then she walked back to Chico and Salina, sneering.

"Animals like you don't even count!" she snarled at them before turning away to enter the tack room. Rapidly, she went over to the grooming stalls, where the names of the horses were displayed on wooden signs, and put the bottle in Rashid's stall where it wouldn't be seen right away. Then, suddenly, she hurried to leave the stable.

"I think we'd better go," she said outside to Cathy. "It's not going to happen today, is it?"

Resigned, Cathy agreed, and walked dejectedly back to the bikes.

"You know what? I think we should come here regularly, so you can get used to everything slowly," suggested Sasha. "Then someday, you'll be able to do it!"

"Do you think so?"

"Of course! C'mon, let's go, before anyone sees us. After all, nobody here has to know you're trying to get your fear under control." Sasha jumped on her bike quickly when she heard several dogs barking inside the house.

"Why not?" asked Cathy, a little puzzled.

"Don't you want to surprise them? Come on!" Without waiting for Cathy's reply, Sasha rode off, and there was nothing for Cathy to do but follow her.

The two of them were only gone a few minutes when Jake came out of his cottage. He walked slowly over to the stable to get the stalls ready for the evening.

*

"Say, Carlotta, how long do you think it'll take before all your stalls are filled?" Kevin asked as he poured himself another glass of cider.

"I can't say exactly, Kevin," Carlotta answered. "Actually, it might be a good sign if most of the stalls stay empty. That would mean that people are actually taking care of their own older animals, rather than having them put down."

"That's true," Ricki agreed. "Which would be really great!"

"But reality can be very different," sighed Lillian, looking out of the window. "When I think about Jonah, and how he was almost put down . . . but to some people horses are just property, just worthless things that can be disposed of when they no longer fill the needs of their owners. It's really awful!"

The others nodded in agreement.

"Thank goodness there are people like you, Carlotta, who not only see the problem but do something about it." Kevin looked over at the owner of Mercy Ranch, who was frowning.

"It's just a drop in the bucket, but still, everyone — young and old — can do something to protect animals, especially the ones that depend on humans for everything."

"And what are you going to do when the stable is full?" asked Ricki. "I mean, we'll come as often as we can, and help with the work in the stalls, but —"

Carlotta interrupted, "I know what you mean. You wonder how I'm going to deal with fifteen stalls a day, alone, including the care and feeding of the horses, when you don't have time to come, don't you?"

"Exactly! Are you going to hire someone?"

"I'll have to," sighed Carlotta, thinking about the already high cost of running the ranch.

"I could leave school in two years and then I could take over the job," suggested Ricki spontaneously. "But what will you do in the meantime?"

Carlotta laughed. "That is a really nice offer, Ricki, but that's definitely not what we're going to do! You're going to get your high school diploma first, and then you're going to college to study for a profession. There are enough people out of work who would be happy to get a job here."

Ricki grimaced. "And if someone is working here who knows nothing about anything, then —?"

Kevin tapped his forehead. "Do you really think Carlotta would hire a stable hand like that?" he asked his girlfriend.

"Of course not," said Carlotta. "You can rest assured that I will look at all the applicants very carefully before choosing. Don't worry! Only someone who gets along with horses and loves animals can work here."

"But how are you going to pay for it? Full time labor costs a lot, doesn't it?" Lillian asked.

"Have I told you about my plan to organize riding clubs for children and young adults? After all, even old animals need a little exercise regularly. One or two hours a day, at a slow pace, won't hurt most older horses at all, if they're healthy." Carlotta looked at her young audience and was amused at the way their mouths hung open in amazement.

"Wow! What a terrific idea!"

"Really? With trail riding and everything?"

"Admit it! You planned all this right from the start, when you first thought about opening a ranch for older horses. Didn't you?"

Carlotta nodded, smiling. "Yes, it's true. I wouldn't have been able to finance it otherwise. Shall I tell you something else? I'm going to put in a small riding ring. Not all of the children who come here will ride well enough to trail ride off the ranch."

Ricki let out a shout. "And we'll be able to ride in the riding ring when we feel like it, won't we?"

"I'll have to think about that," laughed Carlotta. "But *maybe* I'll let you, if you help me with the guests."

"Yeah!" The three friends looked at one another, beaming happily.

"Well, that's enough small talk," decided Carlotta and got up a little awkwardly and glanced at the kitchen clock. "I think it's time for you to be riding back home."

"That is, if we can manage to get Cheryl away from Sheila," Kevin added.

"Oh, my goodness! I completely forgot about her. What did she say, that she only wanted to stay in the stable a few more minutes? Well, a few minutes is certainly a relative concept," exclaimed Carlotta.

Lillian grinned broadly. "Yeah, no kidding! Either relatively long or relatively short."

"That's true, but time doesn't matter when you're dealing with horses," Ricki added.

"Okay, Einstein. Thanks for that insight into the theory of relativity," said Lillian.

"No prob. All right, let's go. It's time for the horses to get their feed anyway."

*

Sheila stood directly in front of Cheryl, who hardly dared to breathe. The girl felt the warm breath of the horse in her hair, and incredible happiness flowed through her.

"Sheila, you are wonderful!" she whispered to her dream horse, and slowly she raised her hand to stroke the animal's neck.

At that moment the howling of a jet plane in the air above

cut through the stable. Startled, Cheryl jumped and pulled back her hand with a hasty movement.

Sheila, who was also startled by the sudden unpleasant noise, bit the girl on the arm.

"Ow!" screamed Cheryl as she got herself out of Sheila's reach with a stumbling step backward. As quickly as she could, she closed the stall door and pushed the bolt through before she pressed her hand on her sore upper arm. With pain showing on her face, she watched Sheila as the horse kicked a few times with her hind hooves, striking the rear wall of the stall.

Jonah, usually so calm, got confused and upset, and watched his stall companion with huge eyes, as Sheila stared in fear at Cheryl, her nostrils flared.

"Oh, it really hurts!" Carefully, the girl pushed up the sleeve of her T-shirt and was shocked as she saw the imprint of the mare's teeth. The bite mark was about four inches long and there were a few drops of blood where Sheila had broken the skin. The arm burned as if it was on fire.

"Hey, Cheryl, are you still in there? Don't tell me you've been standing here the whole time staring at Sheila?" Ricki peered in through the stable door. "Are you coming? We'd better get going." Noticing her friend, Ricki added, "Is something wrong? You look upset."

Cheryl had to fight back her tears. "I'll be right there," she managed to say. "I just want to say good-bye to Sheila."

"All right!" And with that Ricki disappeared again.

Cheryl took a deep breath, blew her nose, and tried to pull the sleeves of her T-shirt down as far as possible to cover up the bite mark. She hoped nobody would notice, especially not Carlotta!

Less than two minutes later she joined the others, who had already attached their snaffles and tightened their saddle girths.

Kevin, who was already sitting in Sharazan's saddle, grinned down at Cheryl. "Was leaving Sheila so hard that it made you cry?"

The girl glared at him and turned to her horse.

"Nope," she answered. "I just had something in my eye, and now it's really burning."

Moving cautiously, she laid the stirrup across the saddle and reached for the saddle girth with both hands so she could tighten it.

"What's that?" asked Carlotta in a sharp tone and reached for Cheryl's arm. She pushed Cheryl's sleeve up, and the bite mark was plainly visible.

Cheryl lowered her head and stared at the ground without any explanation.

"Sheila?" asked Carlotta again, but she didn't really expect an answer. "Didn't I expressly tell you to keep your distance from her? Honey, I have my reasons when I forbid you kids from doing certain things. I've had a lot of experience with horses. Okay, tell me, were you in her stall?" Carlotta stamped her foot. She was furious with herself because she had allowed the girl to stay behind in the stable alone, and furious with Cheryl, who apparently thought that she could ignore her instructions. At the same time, however, she was worried about the girl, whose arm didn't look very good.

Ricki, Kevin, and Lillian exchanged shocked looks.

"I . . . I don't think that Cheryl . . ." began Lillian, who was trying to get Carlotta in a better mood, but one look from Carlotta was enough to silence her.

"I'm sorry," Cheryl stammered. "But it was the noise from the jet plane that startled me, and then I moved too quickly, and Sheila — Oh, Carlotta, she was so sweet before that. She had started to trust me, and she —"

"So you had opened her stall, and you were inside with her?"

With a red face, Cheryl nodded almost imperceptibly.

"Do you understand what could have happened?" Carlotta pressed her lips together, and it was clear by the way her cheek muscles moved that she was having a hard time containing her anger.

"All right," she said a little more calmly. "Come with me. We'll have to treat that arm, and when you get home the first thing you need to do is check your inoculation records to see if your tetanus shots are up to date." Without another word she turned and walked back to the house, and Cheryl followed her like an obedient poodle.

"Yikes!" exclaimed Ricki, her heart beating fast. "Cheryl had better hope that Carlotta doesn't keep her from riding Rashid!"

Lillian nodded. "Yeah. If Carlotta can't trust Cheryl to follow her instructions, she just might. If something were to happen to Rashid while we were out riding . . . I think Carlotta's already had enough drama since Cathy's accident."

"It's really too bad that Sheila bit her. But tell me honestly, wouldn't you have tried to pet Sheila, too, if you'd been alone with her?" When Kevin looked at the two girls, he didn't need an answer.

"Me, too," he said, confirming their looks.

*

A short time later, the friends began their ride back home. Cheryl sat silently in Rashid's saddle, teeth clenched and staring straight ahead.

Ricki was relieved when they were home again. Cheryl took off Rashid's saddle, brushed him hastily, and left the ranch on her bike as quickly as possible.

"Carlotta must have really yelled at her, the way Cheryl was acting."

"You can bet on that."

"But is that any reason to be mad at us? And did you notice, she didn't even clean out poor Rashid's hooves!" Ricki opened the stall door of the dun horse and set about doing Cheryl's job.

"She probably had other things on her mind. Maybe Carlotta really did tell her she couldn't ride Rashid anymore. C'mon, Sharazan, stop it! What's wrong with you?" Kevin gave his roan a little slap on the neck as the animal rubbed his head continuously on the top of the stall divider.

Lillian shook her head. "If he keeps doing that, you can forget about his beautiful long mane."

A little while later, Diablo began to rub his head on Ricki's back, and Holli kept shaking himself and trying to take off his halter by rubbing it on his front legs.

Rashid, Chico, and Salina, however, stood calmly in their stalls and busied themselves eating their hay rations.

"Is it me, or are the three of them acting really weird? Can someone please tell me what's going on?" Ricki stared at her horse, puzzled, as he got more and more agitated.

"I have no idea, but they'll calm down eventually," said Kevin.

"Do you think so? It doesn't look like it."

"How do you feel about biking over to Echo Lake?" asked Lillian, changing the subject. "It's such a beautiful day and I'm so antsy that if I stay inside I might start rubbing myself on the beams, too!"

"Okay, why not. I'll just go let my mom know where we'll be," agreed Ricki, and she ran off.

By the time she got back, the three horses had calmed down a bit and were chewing on their hay contentedly.

Ricki breathed a sigh of relief. "It was probably just some itch caused by sweat underneath the snaffle," she suggested. Then she and Kevin and Lillian went to get their bikes and head to the lake.

*

Cheryl was sitting in Sasha's living room in an angry mood, staring straight ahead.

"I might not be allowed to ride Rashid anymore!" she said, as though her whole problem was Sasha's fault.

That's interesting, thought Sasha devilishly. *This is going better than I'd hoped it would.*

"Well, Cathy will be happy to hear that. I found out that she's been going to Ricki's stable secretly. She probably hopes that she can pay you back somehow, and get Rashid back."

"You're not serious, are you?" Cheryl looked bewildered.

"I swear to you, it's true," affirmed Sasha, a solemn expression on her face.

"So what do I do now?"

"Now you have to make sure that Cathy doesn't do

anything in the next few days to mess things up for you. As far as Rashid is concerned, I think Carlotta will probably have calmed down by tomorrow, and then you should be okay. I doubt she'd look for somebody else to ride her horse."

"Do you really think so?"

"Sure."

"And the thing with Sheila? She didn't even believe me that the mare —"

"Oh, stop talking about that mare. She's not important right now!"

"Yes, she is! That horse is a dream, and I'm not even sure that Carlotta will let me back on the ranch!" Cheryl's eyes started to tear.

"If that mare is so important to you, then you'll have to visit her unofficially," advised Sasha.

"You mean I should go into the stable without asking Carlotta first? I can't do that!"

"Then don't! It was just a suggestion."

"I think I'd better get going. Thanks for listening." Cheryl got up and walked to the door.

"Watch out for Cathy," warned Sasha. "I think she'd do anything to get back at you!"

*

When Cathy got home she was completely depressed, and she threw herself onto her bed and sobbed. She hadn't counted on having such a violent reaction toward Chico and Salina. After a few minutes, however, her misery changed to anger at herself and her fear, and then a stubborn expression appeared on her face.

"Catherine Sutherland, you are such a loser! How are you ever going to ride again if you keep acting like this?" she scolded herself. She got up and walked over to her desk with determination.

"Well, this is for real!" she encouraged herself. This time she managed to clear her mind and, with a new determination, she went to the photo album on her desk and leafed through it with awkward fingers until she came to Rashid's photo.

He still has straw in his mane. Why didn't I notice that when I was taking the picture? she wondered, remembering how long she had worked on grooming her favorite horse.

"You could have told me," she whispered to the photo. Almost automatically, she continued to leaf through the pages, and she realized, to her great joy, that with every photo that she looked at she was becoming calmer and calmer.

You're going to make it! she told herself joyously. *No matter what happens, you're going to ride again!*

*

"Mom, let's just suppose that I was no longer afraid of horses. I'd be allowed to ride again, wouldn't I?" Cathy had decided to ask her mother the big question in front of her father that night at dinner. She watched her parents, who were sitting at the table with her, with the question still in her eyes.

Mrs. Sutherland turned pale and exchanged a quick glance with her husband.

"Cathy, I already told you that —"

"Yeah, yeah, I know! That the evil Rashid caused your

daughter's accident!" exploded Cathy nastily. "But that isn't true, and you know it! My appendix —"

"The appendix didn't throw you, Cathy! But we've already talked about this plenty. I just don't want you to ride!" Mrs. Sutherland's voice sounded final, but Cathy didn't want to give up that easily. She looked over at her father pleadingly.

"Dad, come on, why don't you say something?"

"Well, at the moment, it really doesn't look as if you're going to be able to overcome your fear to get back in the saddle again. You have to admit that," said Mr. Sutherland cautiously.

"I'm not talking about right now. I'm talking about riding in general."

"In general! Okay, let's talk about the facts, the number one fact being that the sport is just too dangerous!" Mrs. Sutherland interrupted.

"But in all the years I was riding, you never had a problem with it!"

"You didn't have an accident in all those years, either!"

Cathy rolled her eyes, and then reached into the back pocket of her jeans to pull out a wrinkled piece of paper that she held out to her mother.

"Here. Read it, please."

"What is this?"

"It's a confirmation from the doctor at the hospital that I could just as easily have fallen off a chair if I'd been on one when my appendix burst!"

"You went back to that doctor? Why?"

"Because I thought you might reconsider the riding issue after you read this." Cathy paced back and forth nervously as her parents read the doctor's report.

114

"See, it wasn't Rashid's fault! And I want to ride again, so much. Well, that is, when . . . when I'm fully recovered from the surgery and finally get rid of this ridiculous fear!" she said quietly.

"Do you really believe that someday you'll be able to touch a horse again, let alone saddle and ride it?" Mr. Sutherland glanced at her skeptically over the top of his glasses. His daughter swallowed hard and gave the slightest nod.

"You don't seem to be convinced of that, or am I wrong?"

"Well, I guess it's going to take a while," admitted Cathy. "But I'm working on it, and I'm already going to the stable to get used to the animals again."

"What? You've been going to the stable? Didn't I expressly forbid you to ever —"

"But Mom, what's the big deal? Ricki —"

"Ricki!" Mrs. Sutherland snorted furiously. "Just as I thought! Your fair-weather friend is behind this!"

"Mom! Please, don't talk about her like that! Anyway, she doesn't have anything to do with this. She doesn't even know that I'm going to the stable. I go there secretly!"

"Secretly! That's just fabulous! This is getting better and better!" Mrs. Sutherland's eyes sparkled with anger.

Cathy's father gently laid a hand on his wife's arm to calm her. "Don't get yourself so upset over this. We can't wrap our daughter in foam rubber just because she was thrown from a horse. I think —"

"You're not serious, are you? 'Just because she was thrown from a horse'? You don't seem to care about your daughter's well-being at all!"

"Up to now, the stable hasn't hurt our daughter, and her

appendix, that unnecessary evil, is gone. I'll be glad when Cathy is back to her old self, unlike you, from the sound of it! You can't keep her away from her friends for the rest of her life just because they ride, and you can't forbid Cathy to do anything that could in any way be dangerous. Look, nowadays it's dangerous just to cross the street!"

"Thank you so much for your support!" hissed Mrs. Sutherland, and she pushed her husband's hand away, furious.

Cathy beamed hopefully at her father. "Does this mean I'm allowed to ride again? I mean, when I'm no longer afraid to?"

"As far as I'm concerned, you can."

"Yes!" Cathy cheered, ran around the table, and gave her father a hug.

"And I'm not even going to be consulted, am I?" Angrily Cathy's mother got up from her chair and silently walked across the room.

"Mom, please —"

At the entrance to the kitchen, Mrs. Sutherland turned to her daughter and glared. "Oh, leave me alone. In this family, everyone does whatever he or she wants anyway. But I'll tell you one thing. Don't bother to come to me afterward complaining about broken bones or sprains or concussions. Your father can deal with things like that in the future!" With these words, Mrs. Sutherland rushed out of the kitchen.

Seconds later, Cathy and her father heard the bedroom door slam shut.

Cathy jumped, but then she smiled at her father. "Do you think that she'll be able to deal with this?"

"Your mother has dealt with much worse, so don't worry

about it." He grinned, and gave his daughter a friendly pat. "Maybe you can get her on your side a little if you clear the table."

"I'll be glad to, for once! Hey, thanks, Dad! You're really — I mean . . . "

"Really great. I know!"

"Exactly!" Cathy quickly arranged the dishes in the dishwasher and put the leftovers into the refrigerator before heading up to her room. "I have to make a call. I can't wait until tomorrow morning to tell someone the good news!"

"Oh, no, and how many hours will you be on the phone, young lady?" groaned Mr. Sutherland.

"I should be finished in twenty minutes."

"I wish," murmured Mr. Sutherland to himself. As he watched his happy daughter walk away, a smile lit his face.

Chapter 8

It was late afternoon, and Carlotta was standing at the paddock gate watching the horses and thinking about the incident between Sheila and Cheryl. It had taken Carlotta considerable time and all the patience she could muster to coax the animal onto the paddock, but she'd managed it, and now Sheila stood as far away from Jonah as she could. She seemed to be permanently on guard, always prepared to flee if she had to.

"What did that Travers man do to you?" Carlotta spoke softly so as not frighten the animal, but nevertheless, at the sound of her words, Sheila's head flew up.

"You'll have to get used to me, girl, or we're going to have a problem." The owner of Mercy Ranch gave her newest arrival a comforting smile. "Look, I'm much smaller than you, and I should be more afraid of you than you are of me. Maybe you should think about that," said Carlotta gently. Then she pushed herself away from the gate and walked slowly back to the house. On her way, she gazed across the driveway.

I'm curious to see if the kids come back today, she thought, and decided to treat herself to a cup of coffee while she waited for them. *Was I too hard on Cheryl?* she asked herself, but then she shook her head firmly. *No! Those youngsters have to learn to follow my instructions. If anything were to happen to any of them, I'd be held responsible.* What she had said to Cheryl was correct, and she was sure that the girl would never ignore her instructions again.

Carlotta heard the phone ring and returned to the house as quickly as possible. Within a few minutes she was sitting in her car, zooming down the driveway toward the road so fast that she left a thick cloud of dust.

*

"This is the life!" Kevin was propped against a tree trunk on the bank of Echo Lake, staring dreamily at the glistening water and the crystal clear sky above. He put his arm around his girlfriend and pulled her closer.

"Well, sweetheart, everything okay?"

Ricki rolled her eyes. "Typical male behavior. What is it you want now?" she said grinning, but she gave her boyfriend an affectionate kiss on the cheek before joining Lillian on the grass.

"What do you two think about Cathy?" asked Lillian sleepily.

"What do you think we think?" Ricki leaned her head on one elbow. "She's become so weird, and her mother keeps having fits, one after the other, and she doesn't want to talk to us. It's a bad situation, and honestly, I'm starting to change my mind about her. I don't feel like supporting her in

119

any way. It doesn't seem to matter what we do, she's always mad at us."

"Do you mean you've decided to write her off?" a curious Lillian asked.

"Oh, no, I can't do that. We've been friends for too long, but I just don't know how we're going to rebuild the friendship if she keeps acting like this."

"Hey, look, Sasha's over there," Kevin noticed, as he stared past Ricki, "and without any boyfriends, for a change."

"Oh, no! Not Sasha!" groaned his girlfriend. "I'm going home."

"Well, why not? We've already had our R and R for the day, and —"

"And I'm starved! Want to go somewhere for a bite to eat?" Lillian opened her eyes and looked hopeful, but Ricki just shrugged her shoulders.

"I can't afford to for the rest of the week. My allowance is almost gone and I need a bag of treats for Diablo, but if you two have too much money and want to invite me, then I won't say no!" She grinned winningly, but Lillian and Kevin were short on cash too.

"Well, then we'll go another time, and this time we'll raid the refrigerator at Cafe Sulai," laughed Ricki. She got up and brushed herself off, sensing Sasha's nasty look on the back of her neck.

"I don't know why, but every time I see that girl I have a really bad feeling."

"Oh, you with your feelings, Ricki," laughed Kevin. "Just ignore her. After all, she's not bothering you!"

"But I can tell she's up to something," insisted Ricki.

"Come on, stop it. The only thing Sasha can do is open her mouth and tell lies. She's incapable of anything else."

"Hmm," responded Ricki as they retrieved their bikes.

"But now that I see Cathy around Sasha so often, it makes me think twice," said Lillian, and indicated behind her with a catty-cornered tilt of her head. "I wouldn't be surprised if she turned up here, too."

"Yeah, I'd be interested in finding out what the two of them have to talk about all of a sudden," commented Kevin.

"Cathy and Sasha are from two different worlds. That friendship won't last long," predicted Ricki, and without another word the three friends got on their bikes and rode slowly home.

They'd left the little woods around Lake Echo, and were already out on the old road when suddenly Carlotta's car passed them in a whirl of dust. It came to an abrupt stop just ahead of them.

"Hi, Carlotta," grinned Kevin, as he stopped beside the car. "You're in a really big hurry, as usual. Where's the fire this time?"

"Well, there's no fire, really, but I forgot about an important meeting at the town hall. The people in the building and zoning department want to talk with me about my driveway . . . whether or not it'll be blacktopped. I'd like to have it blacktopped, otherwise I'm bound to lose my exhaust pipe one of these days on the bumpy stretch."

"Yours or your car's?" joked Kevin.

"Don't be fresh, young man! Say hi to your parents for me, Ricki, and tell your mother that we have to get together for coffee soon."

121

"Okay!"

Carlotta was about to leave, but then she thought of something else. "Ricki, we have to have a talk one of these days."

"What about?"

"I'd like to buy one of your puppies. When you live so far outside of town, as I do, it's a good idea to have a watchdog. Would that be okay with you?" She looked at the girl anxiously.

At first, Ricki turned a little pale and swallowed hard. She sensed that the moment had come for her to say good-bye to the puppies — a thought that she had successfully ignored up to now. However, knowing that no animal could be better off anywhere than with Carlotta, the girl nodded, but with a lump in her throat and her heart thumping.

Carlotta smiled. She knew exactly what her young friend was feeling. "Are you sure?"

Ricki nodded again, before turning away a little, so no one would see her watery eyes.

"Good. Then I'm going to discuss it with your parents in the next few days. Okay, well, now, I really do have to hurry. Take care, all!"

Ricki felt awful, but she joined in Kevin's and Lillian's laughter when Carlotta's car squeaked and groaned as it started off, as though it would break down at any moment.

"She'll drive that car into the ground," exclaimed Lillian, grinning. "I don't think I've ever seen anyone drive like her. Carlotta is really incredible!"

The kids nodded at each other in agreement, and then were on their way again.

"Hey, I think it's great that Carlotta is taking one of the

122

puppies," said Kevin. "At least you know where it'll be going. I would love to take one, but as long as we live in Carlotta's old house we can't. There's no yard, and Mom's always out at Carlotta's ranch taking care of the house." He paused and reflected. Suddenly, he stopped so abruptly that Lillian had to make a sharp turn to avoid running right into him.

"Hey, are you crazy? Why did you stop so suddenly?" she scolded, and Ricki looked at him in astonishment.

"Are you okay?" she asked and stared at his bigger than life grin.

"People, I just had a great idea! If Carlotta would let my mother bring a dog to the ranch during the day, I don't think my mom would have anything against the idea."

"You're not serious, are you?" Ricki looked at her boyfriend. She had to admit that she would like nothing better than for Kevin to have one of the cute puppies.

"Yes, I am. I am absolutely serious. I'll talk with my mom as soon as possible, and if she gives me her okay, then I'm going to work on Carlotta so much that she won't be able to say anything but yes. But maybe we should wait until she has her own puppy. We don't want her to think that our dog would be enough to protect the ranch." The boy winked. Secretly, he already saw himself as a dog owner, and the idea appealed to him a lot.

"That would really be great!" replied Ricki. "Wouldn't it, Lily?" But a glance at Lillian told another story.

"What's wrong, Lily? You're so quiet all of a sudden."

Lillian shrugged her shoulders a little sadly. "I'd love to have Mowgli, but my parents — they're as hard as granite whenever I even mention the word 'dog.'"

"Oh, come on!" Kevin gave the girl a friendly pat on the shoulder. "I promise you that I'll help you talk your parents into it. We'll think of some way to convince them."

"That's what you think. If my dad doesn't want to do something, then nobody can change his mind!" Lillian sighed.

"And what about your mother? Couldn't we work on her?" asked Ricki, who was beginning to like the idea of giving all of the dogs to hers friends.

"I think it would be easier to talk my mom into it."

"See!" Kevin beamed. "We'll keep at your mother until she gives in."

"And then?"

"Then, hopefully, we'll prove my grandmother right," joked Kevin. "She always used to say, 'The man may be the head of the family, but the woman is the neck that turns the head'."

Ricki looked at Lillian and the two girls burst out laughing.

"That's great! Actually, it should even make sense to your father, Lily. If we manage to convince your mother, then we'll almost have won," said Ricki.

"Hmm," said Lillian. "That would really be great! Well, we can at least try. You can't win without trying."

"So true."

The three happy friends got back on their bikes and finally headed for Ricki's house. Kevin couldn't wait to play with his favorite puppy and tell him that he was going to have a new home soon.

*

"Hey, that sounds just great," Sasha yelled into her cell phone, making a fist with her free hand. Cathy had called her right away in her happiness and reported the good news. Darn! If Cathy was really making such good progress overcoming her fear, she, Sasha, could forget her whole plan . . . although . . . well, anyway, she was going to do everything she could to get back at the whole group of friends.

No one is going to call me a liar and get away with it, repeated Sasha again to herself, and she tried to end the conversation with Cathy as quickly as possible. She needed time to rethink the whole plan.

She slowly packed up her cell phone, makeup case, sunglasses, bottle of water, and the latest copy of *Seventeen*. She didn't feel like hanging out at the lake anymore, especially since none of her friends were here. Just as she was about to close the zipper on her bag she discovered one of Cheryl's barrettes, which she had borrowed a long time ago. Pensively, she picked it up, and suddenly had an idea.

Just wait, she thought, and her face changed to a self-satisfied grin. *That old lady Mancini won't let you ride for long, Cheryl, I promise you!* She quickly put the barrette into her pants pocket and got on her bike, and then rode as fast as she could down the bumpy path through the woods. She was pretty sure this trail would lead her straight to Carlotta's ranch.

*

When Ricki and her friends arrived at the Sulais' house, they were immediately surrounded by the dogs, who greeted them merrily.

Kevin's favorite puppy kept jumping up on him and almost made him fall off of his bike.

"You little devil, you," he said, laughing loudly. "At least let me get off of my bike first!" He carelessly leaned his bike against the house so he could give all of his attention to the little dog, while Lillian let Mowgli lick her hands and Ricki divided her attention between Rosie and the other puppy.

"Have you two noticed that this guy has a white beard?" asked Kevin, completely out of breath.

Ricki grinned. "Well, let's hope it doesn't grow as long as Gandalf's beard in Lord of the Rings."

Kevin hesitated. "Gandalf! That's great! Ricki, can we name him Gandalf? I think that would be really cool," he pleaded.

His girlfriend laughed. "That's okay with me. The name suits him. Now all we need is a name for this little cutie here," Ricki said, looking at Rosie's third son. "It looks as though he's going to be the one to go to Carlotta. Do you have any idea what name she might like?"

"Hmm. Let me think . . . Well, he'll be a lucky puppy to have such a happy home. We could name him Lucky or Happy — or something like that," suggested Lillian after thinking it over for a short time.

"I like the name Lucky. And besides, Carlotta could use some more luck for her ranch. That's a good idea, Lily!" Ricki clapped her hands enthusiastically, which made Lucky jump up on her again and again. "I think he likes the name, too! And to think, I worried over the names for weeks!"

"Well, if you'd just asked us at the beginning, then the poor little things wouldn't have had to run around nameless so long. I —" Kevin hadn't even finished his sentence when Jake came out of the stable door with a serious look on his face.

"Hey, Jake, what's up?" Ricki called happily to the old stable hand. Then she noticed his stone-hard expression.

"Did something happen?" Startled, she walked toward him.

"What did you do to the horses today?" the old man thundered suddenly.

"Why? I don't understand. What's wrong?"

"What's wrong? Go inside and look at the mess!"

Ricki exchanged a startled look with her friends, and all three took off. Seconds later they were standing in front of their horses with looks of disbelief on their faces.

"Good grief, what is that?" Ricki stared at Diablo's head, while Lillian and Kevin examined their animals.

Jake had taken the halters off of the horses, except for Rashid, Chico, and Salina, and stared angrily at the kids.

"This is just awful!" he hissed. "How can you miss seeing something like this? Your horses are completely rubbed raw behind their ears and around their muzzles, and you don't even think it's important enough to wipe off the blood and rub in a salve! You have more important things to do, have you? And I always thought that you were mature enough to take responsibility for your own horses. It looks like I was dead wrong about you — all of you!" Furious, he glared at Ricki. "If I had thought that you would care so little for Diablo, I would never have given him to you!"

Ricki turned pale as she approached her beloved horse, her knees shaking. There were open wounds that were bleeding.

"Jake," she began softly. "I don't know what's going on here, but when we left it wasn't like this! Honestly, it wasn't!"

"Oh, it wasn't?"

"NO!" Ricki shook her head wildly.

"And how do you explain this disaster? What did you do to these horses?"

"We didn't do anything, Jake," Kevin joined in, while Lillian examined Holli's neck with worry and concern.

"This just isn't possible! It can't be!" she mumbled to herself. Against Holli's white coat, the bloody scabs and spots were especially visible.

Sharazan wasn't quite so bad, which made Kevin less anxious, at least as far as his horse was concerned. He glanced over at the dun horse in the next stall.

"At least Rashid seems to be okay," he said, and Jake nodded emphatically.

"Yes! I'd say that the new girl in your group is the only one who takes good care of her horse!" he continued to scold.

Ricki took a deep breath. "Jake, you're being unfair. And anyway, Cheryl didn't even take the time to clean out Rashid's hooves today before she left. If that's what you mean by 'taking care' of something, then I guess you're right."

"Yeah, yeah," growled the old man. "But at least Rashid isn't standing in his stall bleeding!"

"We have to disinfect these wounds," said Lillian, and was already on her way to the tack room, but Jake just shook his head.

"Don't bother! I already did. Who knows how they'd look if I hadn't!"

"Well, it can't be a form of eczema, or it wouldn't have happened to all three horses at once," suggested Lillian.

"That much is true. You should know where it came from!" Jake was still just as upset as when they'd arrived, and Ricki began to worry about his bad heart.

"Please, Jake, don't get so upset, it's not good for you!" she pleaded with him, but every new thing she said just made the old man madder.

"You kids are totally irresponsible!" he thundered. "Just get out of here, and don't come back until you tell me what happened!"

"Excuse me, Jake, but you can't keep us away from our own horses," Kevin dared to object, but faced with the stable hand's furious look, the boy backed down.

"They should be taken away from you!" he spat out and pointed to the stall door. "Get out!"

Sullen, the three friends glanced at each other before they slunk past Jake toward the exit, their heads hanging with dejection. Of course they could understand the old man, whose entire life was devoted to horses, but it really hurt that Jake had so little trust in them.

"If I catch the person responsible for this, I'll kill him," murmured Ricki, her voice trembling, when they were outside the stable.

"Who can it be? And we don't even have any clues about what he or she was trying to do." Kevin shrugged his shoulders despondently.

"But we know that it isn't anything we did. We groomed our animals just like always, went riding, and afterwards, we took care of them, just like always, and then suddenly, and almost simultaneously, they began to rub their heads."

Lillian bit her lips. "And interestingly, Rashid doesn't have any problem at all. Well, okay, Chico and Salina don't either, but they weren't with us when we went riding. It must have something to do with the ride, but what?"

"Don't ask me. It's more than just mysterious. But you know what makes me mad? That Jake is acting like it's our fault. He should know that something weird is going on."

"Well, I'm sure he knows that. But he thinks that we had something to do with it."

"That's crazy! As though we would ever let our horses get in that condition. Really!"

"So what should we do now?"

"I have no idea. I'm going to my room to think about it. Don't be mad at me," Ricki added, looking at her two friends.

"Of course we won't. I'm going home, too," Kevin said.

"Me, too. This whole thing has really freaked me out!" responded Lillian, and she turned toward her bike.

"Okay, see you tomorrow," said Ricki, before she turned and disappeared into the house.

Chapter 9

Sasha arrived at Mercy Ranch brooding and impatient. She had rehearsed exactly what she wanted to say to Carlotta, but Carlotta wasn't home yet.

That's okay, thought the girl, and while she waited for Carlotta she went over to the stable to get a look inside. Grudgingly she had to nod in admiration when she saw all the well-lit, spacious stalls. Then she turned away quickly and ran over to the paddock, where Jonah and Sheila were standing.

"So you're the wonderful Sheila who bit Cheryl?" Sasha grinned. "You did a great job. She deserved it!" She stuck her hand in her jeans pocket and pulled out the barrette. She looked at the hair accessory for a moment, and then she stretched out her arm and let it fall onto the paddock.

So, Cheryl, she thought, *this should end your future with Rashid once and for all!*

Sasha heard a car motor in the distance, so she turned away hastily and hurried back to her bike.

By the time Carlotta stopped her car and got out, surprised to see the teenager at Mercy Ranch, Sasha had managed to put on a dejected, downcast look.

"What are you doing here?" asked Carlotta, with a wary tone in her voice. She hadn't liked Sasha from the beginning.

"Hello, Mrs. Mancini. I just want to apologize to you for what I said about the old horses. I didn't mean it the way it sounded," she said, trying to sound convincing.

Carlotta's eyes narrowed a little. *Why, you little faker,* she thought, as Sasha looked at her pleadingly.

"I'm sorry! Really I am!"

"And what do you want from me now? That I take away Cheryl's riding privileges with Rashid and give them to you instead?"

Sasha raised her hands defensively and put on a winning smile.

"No, no, Mrs. Mancini, I know that isn't possible anymore, but . . . well, I don't know how I should say this."

Carlotta leaned a little more heavily on her crutch. "What do you want to say?"

Sasha pretended to be uneasy. "Well, Cheryl told me what happened with Sheila, and I know that I'm talking behind my girlfriend's back right now, but I'm afraid that something could happen to her again."

"At the moment, I don't understand you," responded Carlotta a little impatiently. "Maybe you could make your point a bit more clearly?"

"Yes, excuse me, but this is really hard for me. Well, Cheryl told me that she's not allowed to go near Sheila anymore, and that after what happened you might take away her riding privileges with Rashid. Anyway, she said that she's going to visit Sheila anyway, in secret, and . . ."

Carlotta was silent. Something told her that she shouldn't believe anything this girl said, but at the same time she felt anger rising in her toward Cheryl. She could easily imagine the girl trying to continue to visit Sheila.

"I'm very sure that she was here at the ranch today," added Sasha.

"Of course she was here, she was bitten!"

"That's not what I mean! She said that she was going to see Sheila again today in order to show her that she wasn't afraid of her."

"What? I don't believe it!" Carlotta shook her head. That seemed unlikely to her. After what happened, Cheryl wouldn't dare come back, at least not today.

"Whatever. I just wanted to tell you. I have no idea if she was here or if she's coming later. But I'm just afraid that something could happen to her again, and that's why I told you all of this." Sasha turned toward her bike and got on it. "I'm leaving now. 'Bye, Mrs. Mancini. I hope you don't tell on me, otherwise my friendship with Cheryl would be ruined, and that would really make me sad."

Since Carlotta didn't answer, Sasha just shrugged her shoulders and rode off.

Carlotta watched her go for a long while before she sighed and then went over to the paddock. It was time to return the horses to the stable, and she figured that getting Sheila back into her stall was going to take some time — and a lot of gentle coaxing.

133

As she bent down to slide through the paddock fence, she saw Cheryl's barrette. "Where did this thing come from?" she asked herself as she picked it up and looked at it suspiciously. Suddenly it all became clear to her.

"Unbelievable! Don't tell me that Sasha was right!" Carlotta put the barrette into her pocket, her face clouded with anger. *Tomorrow, Cheryl will have to answer for this,* she thought.

*

At school the next day, Cathy looked over at Ricki cautiously. Ricki had gotten used to ignoring her desk companion so that she didn't have to listen to her insulting comments.

But Cathy had a guilty conscience as far as her former friend was concerned, and she felt she had to tell Ricki how hard she was trying to find her way back to her life of riding and horses. On the other hand, it always hurt her when she saw how happy Ricki, Lillian, and Kevin seemed to be when they were with Cheryl.

I should tell her that I was in the stable, thought Cathy, but she knew that Ricki wouldn't exactly be happy about it, after Cathy had acted the way she had. But the girl noticed that Ricki was distracted today, that her thoughts were somewhere else. When Mr. Reid asked her a question, she just looked straight through him.

"Oh, Miss Sulai has decided to daydream again today? I hope you have a good rest, Ricki!"

Something is wrong with her, but it would be weird if I asked her about it. Cathy sighed quietly, and began to copy the assignment from the board, while Ricki continued to stare into space.

"Hey, believe me." Sasha had managed to get Cheryl to the most secluded corner of the school grounds. "Cathy's been going to your stable secretly. She said that Ricki and her friends can expect something to happen — 'consequences' was her word — after they just dropped her like that!"

"What? Are you sure?"

"Of course I'm sure, or I wouldn't be telling you. Hey, I've got to go. See you later!" Sasha ran off quickly before her former friend could ask her any more questions.

Furious, Cheryl watched her go. "That is unbelievable!" she murmured and hurried back to inform Ricki, Kevin, and Lillian, who were standing under the big oak tree, engaged in serious conversation.

"Hey! What's up? Want to hear some news?" Cheryl quickly joined her friends.

"No, not really," answered Ricki dryly. At the moment, she just didn't feel like gossiping about any of her classmates.

"Maybe you would, if you knew that —" began Cheryl, but even Kevin stopped her.

"It doesn't matter what you have to say, we have other problems at the moment," he said seriously.

"How come? What's wrong?" asked Cheryl, curious now, and Lillian told her about the mysterious illness that afflicted the horses.

"That's terrible! Really! I'm glad, though, that it didn't happen to Rashid too."

"Yeah, luckily, but we're still trying to figure out how it could have happened. Jake almost tore our heads off. I bet someone's messing with us. This can't be normal. If only I knew who it was!" Ricki breathed in loudly.

Cheryl swallowed excitedly. Maybe Cathy —? "I think you guys should hear what I have to say after all. Maybe it will give you a clue. Well, I just talked with Sasha, and . . . "

When Cheryl had finished telling them her story, the three friends looked at each other, completely baffled.

"You mean that Cathy may have done something bad?" asked Kevin.

"I don't mean anything at all. I'm just telling you what Sasha told me."

"I don't believe it!" Lillian shook her head firmly. "Sasha lies every time she opens her mouth. Cathy wouldn't do anything like this! She loves horses too much to hurt them in any way, don't you think, Ricki? After all, you've known her much longer than the rest of us."

"I can't imagine it either, but remember the fire at the riding hall? She —"

"She was just an unwilling accomplice. Lark talked her into it," Kevin said, coming to Cathy's defense.

"Yeah, but think about it. Why did it just affect our horses and not Rashid? That's what makes me wonder about it," said Ricki. "To be honest, I can believe that she's capable of doing such a thing. When Cathy's jealous, she freaks out. I'm just going to ask her about it. Then I'll see how she reacts!" And with that, she went to look for Cathy.

"Oh, man, did you see Ricki's face? There's going to be trouble. I think we'd better go after her," exclaimed Lillian to the two others, and they all quickly went to catch up with their friend.

Ricki was heading directly toward Cathy, who she had seen standing beside the school entrance. With every yard that she got closer, Ricki felt anger rising within her. Suddenly, she was convinced that Cathy was the reason her darling Diablo had to suffer with those wounds, and that made her almost crazy.

Startled, Cathy jumped when she saw Ricki, whose face was red with anger, confronting her.

"Cathy, we have to talk, and don't even think about running away from me, like you've been doing for quite a while now every time you see me! Were you in our stable? What did you do to our horses? Why did you do it? We didn't do anything to you!" The words flowed out of Ricki in a torrent, and she didn't even give Cathy a chance to answer her.

The girl turned pale and took a step back because Ricki looked as though she could jump on her anytime.

"I didn't do anything!" Cathy answered, her voice shaking, as her thoughts raced through her head. *The horses? What's wrong with them? What is Ricki talking about?*

"So! You didn't do anything? Then why did you go into our stable secretly? You could have at least asked if we minded," Ricki countered immediately.

Something blew up inside Cathy. She felt hurt that her old girlfriend actually thought that she had done something to the horses. *Ricki couldn't really believe that — or could she?* Cathy raised her head stubbornly a little higher and said firmly, "I wasn't in your stable and I haven't even seen your horses from a distance. Who said that I did?" *Sasha!* The idea went through her head right after the question. *That rat!*

"Oh, sure," Ricki said accusingly. "You say you don't know anything? Just as I thought. Let me remind you of the fire at the riding hall. You said you didn't know anything about that either! Is it like that again? Are you trying to cover up something? Cathy, you are really a disappointment! I'll just say one more thing. If it is your fault that our horses are standing in their stalls covered with raw, bloody, itchy spots, you're going to have more trouble than you've ever had in your life! I promise you that! And understand this. I'm going to find out who the responsible person is!"

For a moment, Cathy couldn't breathe. *Bloody spots? Rashid?*

"What did you say? And Rashid? Does he also have —?"

Ricki just snorted cynically. "Oh, come on! You made sure that your darling wouldn't be hurt! That one thing shows me that you had something to do with it! You still can't stand the fact that we're out having fun riding and you lost Rashid to Cheryl! Otherwise, I just can't explain why you're acting so weird with us!"

Other students had gradually noticed the loud argument between the two girls and started to gather around Cathy and Ricki.

"You can't imagine how angry I'm feeling right now! I could —!" Ricki turned abruptly and pushed her way through the crowd.

Kevin and Cheryl looked at Cathy for a long time before they followed Ricki. Only Lillian stayed behind for a moment and stared at Cathy pensively.

"Cathy, what you're doing is really stupid," she said just loud enough for the girl to hear.

"But I haven't done anything," she answered, close to tears. "Ricki is blaming me for things that I never did. Please, believe me."

Lillian gave her one more sad glance, but then she turned aside, too, and went away. She didn't know what — or whom — to believe.

Cathy became even more upset when she heard what people around her were whispering.

"That's just the kind of person she is!"

"I've always thought she was capable of something like that!"

"Those poor horses!"

"What a mean girl!"

Cathy closed her eyes for a moment and breathed deeply. Then she raced up the front steps to the school as quickly as she could to get away from the sneering, unsympathetic looks of the other students.

Sasha! The name thundered continually inside her head. *Why did you do it? And I thought we were friends.*

*

When Ricki got home from school, the first thing she did was go to the stable to see how the horses were doing. She sighed with relief when she saw that the skin under their coats was no longer as red as it was the day before and the sores had healed a bit.

Jake, who had come into the stable right after Ricki, punished her by pretending that she wasn't there.

"Jake, don't be like that! This mess isn't our fault at all! It looks like Cathy was here secretly and did something to the horses. I found out today at school." Ricki tried to defend herself and her friends, but the old stable hand just looked at her with pity.

"Oh, so now Cathy is the guilty one. Ricki, I'm ashamed of you. Can't you think of any better excuse than to blame your friend, who, in her present state of fear couldn't possibly get that close to a horse? You should be ashamed of yourself. I completely misjudged you." After staring at the girl for a long time, Jake disappeared into the tack room shaking his head.

"Darn it, he's right!" she had to admit to herself. She had totally overreacted and probably humiliated Cathy in front of her classmates. *Oh, man, why didn't I think things over first before I opened my big mouth? I bet she's feeling awful,* she thought and sat down despondently on a bale of straw and buried her face in her hands.

*

Ricki, Kevin, and Lillian were already grooming their horses that afternoon when Cheryl arrived.

"Hey, have you been here long? What's going on? How are our three poor invalids, any better?" Curious, she went from one stall to the next to examine Holli, Sharazan, and Diablo.

"They really do look better, but we definitely can't go riding just yet. The snaffles would rub against their muzzles and re-injure them," replied Lillian.

Cheryl nodded in agreement, although she was disappointed. She would have loved to go riding on Rashid.

"What do you think?" she asked hesitantly. "Could I go riding alone for about a half hour?"

Kevin grinned. "As long as you don't take along a hot-air balloon, I don't think it would be a problem. Rashid is fine by himself."

"Yeah, go ahead. It doesn't make any sense for you not to ride when he's completely okay." said Lillian, and Ricki nodded.

"Great!" Cheryl beamed brightly and hurried into the

tack room to get her grooming kit. She gave Rashid a quick grooming, then she saddled him quickly and rode off. She didn't want to waste any time with this wonderful horse.

For a moment, she considered riding over to Carlotta's ranch, but she changed her mind immediately. First of all, it would take her half an hour to get there, and secondly, she wasn't so sure that it was a good idea to come into contact with Carlotta again so soon.

"No, my sweetheart," she said, grinning, and she patted Rashid's neck. "I don't think I'm going to do that to myself today!"

*

Ricki ran out of the tack room screaming.

"Help! There's a huge spider in Rashid's grooming box! Kevin, please, can you get that creature out of there, otherwise I can't go back into the tack room!" Ricki was standing in front of her boyfriend with a pleading look on her face, and he was laughing out loud.

"Say it!" he teased. "Say it out loud! Right now!"

Ricki rolled her eyes but she submitted to her fate. "My brave hero! My rescuer! My whatever, just hurry before it decides to go someplace else to ambush me! Please, Kevin, hurry up!" Ricki's skin crawled at the mere thought of spiders, but the boy had already disappeared into the tack room. In a few seconds he came back to the corridor with the box of grooming tools in his hands.

"I decided to save its life," he said dramatically as he took the box outside and emptied it onto the narrow strip of grass in front of the house. An eight-legged "black monster" scuttled out of the box and disappeared in the grass.

141

Why do girls always have to exaggerate? Kevin wondered as he put the tools back into the box. Suddenly, he hesitated. What kind of bottle was that, that had rolled to the side? Curious, he picked it up, but there was no label on it.

"Hmm," he said, and he took off the cap to smell the contents. "Phew, that stinks! What is this stuff?" he called out and motioned for Lillian and Ricki to come.

"Do you two have any idea what this could be? I just found it in Rashid's grooming box."

"Give it to me." Ricki stuck out her hand for it, and made a face, too, when she smelled it. She shook her head. "No idea! Lily? What do you think?"

After the sixteen-year-old had smelled the contents several times, her face brightened.

"It smells like the stuff the hairdresser put on my hair when I got that ridiculous perm," she said, laughing. "I can't imagine Cheryl wanting to wave Rashid's mane!"

The friends looked at each other and grinned, but all of a sudden Ricki turned serious.

"That's it!"

"What's it?"

"That stuff! I remember reading an article in one of my mom's magazines about a woman who had an allergic reaction to the solution hairdressers use for permanents. Her whole head was covered with sores and pimples, and her hair even started to fall out. The photos looked awful. I'll bet anything someone put this stuff on the horses!"

The three friends were silent as they looked at each other.

"That's possible, but I don't think Holli, Sharazan, and Diablo would have stood still with that awful smell. Holli tries to hide in a corner when he smells even a trace of lotion on my hands," exclaimed Lillian.

"If this stuff is concentrated, then it could easily have that effect! But you're right – how did somebody manage to get the horses to stand still?" Ricki's voice shook. She was sure now that she had wrongly accused her former friend. "Well, one thing is clear . . . Cathy couldn't have done it. But who, then? Oh, this is driving me crazy!"

Kevin was staring at the little bottle as though it could tell him what had happened. Suddenly, he hit his forehead with his hand.

"Hey, you guys, I just thought of something!" he shouted and ran back into the tack room, followed by the girls. He grabbed one of the halters and examined the inside closely.

"Can you please tell me what you're doing?" Ricki asked impatiently.

"Aha! That's how it was done!" Paying no attention to his girlfriend, he sniffed the other halters and found an almost imperceptible trace of the smell of the perm solution.

"Smell this. Do you notice anything? And look closely. The halters are smeared in the nose and neck areas inside, and you can still smell that stuff." He held the halters up to the girls, inviting them to smell.

Ricki turned pale. "That's incredible! Really! That means someone rubbed the stuff onto the halters, and they probably did it while we were out riding! Well, then it could have been Cathy. I mean, she's probably not afraid of halters."

"It's possible," agreed Lillian. "We should call her and ask her to come here. Maybe she'll admit it when she sees the condition of the poor horses."

"Okay, let's do it. I'll call her right now and tell her that we need to talk with her again. Let's hope she comes." Ricki raced off.

"If she doesn't, we can consider that an admission of guilt," Kevin called after her. "I bet she'll come," he then said to Lillian. "She won't want anyone to think that it's her fault that the horses are suffering!"

*

Carlotta had decided to drive to the Sulais' stable. She hoped to find Cheryl there and ask her about the barrette. She also wanted to talk to Ricki's mother about buying one of the puppies.

She got to the house about the same time as Cathy, who was just leaning her bike against the wall.

A happy smile formed on Carlotta's face as she got out of the car. "Cathy! What a surprise. I haven't seen you in such a long time! How are you? Child, I'm so glad to see you at the stable again!" She hugged the girl warmly, but when she felt Cathy's rejection she let go of her immediately.

"You're still mad at me because of Rashid, aren't you?" she asked quietly, but Cathy just shook her head.

"No, not really," she said sadly. "Ricki thinks I did something to the horses, and —"

"You? That's ridiculous!" Carlotta made a face. "Where are those kids? In the stable? Come with me, we'll take a look."

Cathy hesitated. "The horses are in the stable. I'm not sure I can —"

Carlotta understood. She put her arm around the girl protectively and drew her close. "Don't be afraid, Cathy. I'm with you. I won't let anything happen to you."

Cathy swallowed. She trusted Carlotta completely, and the older woman's protective arm gave her a feeling of security.

"Come on. You'll see. It's not as bad as you think. You'll make it, but you have to take the first step."

Cathy remembered the panic that had overtaken her when she saw Chico and Salina, but she knew that if anyone could help her to overcome her fear, Carlotta could.

"Okay," she whispered quietly, thankful that Carlotta's arm held her even more tightly.

"Then come!" With a gentle pressure, Carlotta urged Cathy forward until they were both standing in the doorway to the stable. But when she saw the huge horses, Cathy began to shake.

"We'll stay right here, my dear," Carlotta said, sensing the girl's fear. "Take all the time you need to get accustomed to the animals again."

Ricki, Kevin, and Lillian were just leaving the house and walking over to the stable. They were glad to see Carlotta, but when they noticed Cathy their faces hardened a little. Ricki felt guilty about the accusations she'd made toward her friend in the schoolyard, but the possibility that Cathy had rubbed perm solution on the halters didn't make her exactly friendly.

"Hi, Carlotta. It's good to see you. Do you want to look at the puppy?"

"*The* puppy? Aren't the others here anymore?"

Kevin and Lillian turned pink and looked at each other.

"Well," Ricki said slowly, "they're all still here, but it's like this: Kevin and Lilly already selected the ones they want if . . . if they can persuade their parents."

Carlotta began to laugh. "Well, why should your mother have anything against dogs, Kevin? She loves animals, and Lillian, your parents have a huge farm, so there can't really be a problem, can there?"

Lillian shrugged her shoulders. "I've tried to talk with them about it, but Dad —"

"Your father? Oh, come on! Anyone who saves a donkey from a circus can be persuaded to take a dog. You know what, when we're finished here, I'll go to your house and talk to your parents about it. I'll be surprised if you don't have a new farm dog soon."

Lillian beamed. If there was anyone, besides her mother, who could convince her father, it was Carlotta. "Thank you, Carlotta, you are so great!"

Kevin stammered around a little. "Well, Mom would probably be okay with it, but it's not just her decision, exactly," he said, hesitating.

Carlotta looked at him, puzzled. "Who else's, then?"

"Well . . . yours! Mom is at your ranch more often than anywhere else, and she'd have to take the dog with her when she works at your place."

"I see. So what's the problem?" asked Carlotta.

Kevin gave her a huge hug. "Are you serious?" he asked, beaming.

"Of course! As far as I'm concerned, always! But now, tell me. What's going on with the horses?"

"Rashid isn't here," whispered Cathy just then.

"Cheryl went riding with him. He's the only one who doesn't have ugly sores," said Lillian, walking over to Holli and pointing to his scabby hide.

Carlotta let go of Cathy immediately and went to look at the animals more closely.

Ricki's face darkened. With a side-glance, she stared at Cathy without saying a word. But then she walked over to Carlotta and started to tell her everything, starting with Jake's accusations, including her fit at school, and she ended it by suggesting that Cathy had something to do with it, while Kevin brought the little bottle of liquid as proof.

After everything had been said, Carlotta was silent for a long time, during which she stared at Cathy, who had tears running down her cheeks.

"I swear I had nothing to do with this," she repeated. "I admit that I lied at school when I said that I wasn't here, but Ricki was so mad. And it's true that I was here once yesterday afternoon. I hoped to overcome my fear of horses by standing in front of them. Chico and Salina were the only ones here, but the sight of them was enough to drive me out of the stable. But I didn't do anything! I swear it! I could never do something like that!"

"I believe you," Carlotta said comfortingly to her. She knew people well, and she was positive that Cathy was telling the truth.

"But who was it, then?" Ricki raised her hands in desperation. Now they were back at square one!

"Hey, I just thought of something." Lillian swallowed excitedly. "Cheryl's mother is a hairdresser. That means that stuff like this is in her house."

Ricki turned pale. "Cheryl? You don't really believe that, do you? Why should she do something like this?"

"Maybe to put suspicion on Cathy, so Cathy would never

147

have another chance to ride Rashid. After all, the bottle was hidden in the bottom of *his* grooming box," added Kevin.

"And when is she supposed to have done this? She was with us on the ride," Ricki reminded them.

"Didn't she go back into the stable before we left, because, supposedly, she'd forgotten her cell phone? She could have put that stuff on the halters then."

"Well, we can ask her now. She just got back," reported Lillian.

Cathy turned around quickly and stared trembling at the sight of Rashid.

There he was, as big as life, and looking back at her before he greeted her with a friendly whinny.

Cheryl noticed that Cathy was there, and her stomach cramped up. What did she want?

Rashid didn't want to stand still so that Cheryl could loosen his girth, and he was glad when he was finally led toward the stable and toward Cathy, but then he stopped suddenly.

"Come on!" urged Cheryl, but the horse stood still a few yards away from Cathy.

Hey, what's going on? he seemed to ask. *Where have you been all this time?*

Cathy swallowed excitedly when she saw that Rashid was scraping his hoof disobediently.

"Come!" Cheryl's firm voice cut through the tense atmosphere, but Rashid just didn't want to follow her into the barn. He began to move toward Cathy, pulling Cheryl with him. Cathy couldn't back away from him anymore, because she stood with her back to the wall of the house.

There were pearls of cold sweat on Cathy's forehead, and suddenly Carlotta was at her side with her arm around her.

"Don't be afraid, child!" she whispered. "He just wants to greet you. He must have missed you terribly, poor boy!"

Rashid stopped just in front of her. Cathy felt she was going to faint, and she closed her eyes.

Please, please, go away! she thought, frightened, but then she felt the warm breath of the horse on her face, and then the gentle, soft lips nuzzling her body, looking for a treat.

Carlotta stroked Cathy's tense arm, took her trembling hand, and put it very carefully on Rashid's forehead.

Suddenly tears began rolling down Cathy's cheeks.

"I missed you so much, too," she said softly, and, sobbing, she leaned against Rashid's neck and cried away all the fear of the past few weeks.

When Carlotta saw that Cathy was cuddling closer and closer into the horse, she took the reins from Cheryl's hand and gave them to Cathy.

"Bring him into the stable when you're ready," she said sweetly. Then she gestured for Cheryl to come with her.

*

It was an unpleasant conversation for Rashid's new rider.

"You don't really believe that, do you?" Cheryl couldn't understand what they were saying, and kept repeating, just like Cathy, that she was innocent.

All of a sudden, Carlotta pulled out the barrette. "Tell me, do you recognize this?" she asked, and Cheryl nodded, puzzled.

"Of course, it's mine. Where did you find it?"

"In my paddock. Didn't I tell you to stay away from Sheila?"

"Yes, of course you did. And that's what I did!"

"You were on the paddock while I wasn't home!"

"No, I wasn't!"

"Then how did your barrette get there?"

"I don't know! And anyway, it's impossible! I haven't worn that thing for a long time!" Cheryl ran her fingers through her hair. She couldn't understand why everything had turned against her suddenly. But all at once, she held her breath.

"Sasha! A long time ago, I lent Sasha this barrette. I completely forgot!" she shouted.

Carlotta raised her eyebrows. "Sasha? She came to see me yesterday and told me that you wanted to visit Sheila against my orders."

Cheryl shook her head wildly. "That's not true! It was she who said that I should do that, if Sheila meant so much to me! Maybe she threw the barrette onto the paddock to make it look like I was ignoring your instructions again. Maybe she wanted to make sure that I wouldn't be allowed to ride anymore. Ever since I've had riding privileges with Rashid, she's been acting really weird."

Cathy, who was just entering the stable with Rashid, listened closely, and suddenly everything became clear to her.

"Hey, I have to tell you guys something. Sasha came with me to the stable, and she was alone in here for a while, after I ran out. Maybe *she* doctored the halters."

"But how did she get hold of perm solution?" asked Kevin.

Cheryl said, "My mother gave her mother a perm at her house a while ago, and left a bottle there by accident. I was supposed to return it ages ago, but I kept forgetting. Can I see it?"

Kevin showed Cheryl the little bottle, and she nodded emphatically. "That's it! That's one of the bottles my mother uses when she gives perms."

"Well, what do you know? Everything suddenly seems clear," Carlotta nodded seriously. "I'm going to call her mother and discuss all of this with her. Sasha seems to be a really sly little beast!"

"Oh, yeah!" The friends all nodded in agreement, while Cathy continued to focus on Rashid. Still a little unsure of herself, but without fear, she dealt with the saddle tack and wouldn't let anyone stop her from brushing his coat.

Cheryl watched her sadly. She had sensed that somehow Cathy would get Rashid back, but she felt that it was right, even though it hurt.

Carlotta looked at both girls before she cleared her throat and said, "Well, I'm not an idiot. I know what's going on inside both of you right now. You're asking yourselves which one of you will be allowed to ride Rashid, aren't you?"

Cathy and Cheryl looked at each other shyly and then they both nodded.

Carlotta smiled. "Well, it's a difficult situation, but I think I have a solution that will make both of you happy. Cathy, I'm giving Rashid back to you, officially, as of now, provided that your parents don't object."

Cathy gave a little suppressed cry of joy and wrapped her arms around Rashid as Cheryl's eyes filled with tears of disappointment.

"And Cheryl may get accustomed to Sheila, but for right now, only when I'm around!" said Carlotta. "When you've won her trust, then you may ride her."

Sheila! She would have Sheila to take care of and ride! Her greatest dream! Cheryl could hardly believe her luck, and she gave Carlotta a huge hug.

"Thank you, thank you, thank you!" she stammered again and again.

"And the other great thing is that the horse's condition isn't contagious," grinned Lillian and she gave Carlotta a thumb's-up. "Bulls-eye!"

Just then Jake entered the stable. Curious about all the commotion, he looked from one person to the other, and then finally asked, "What's going on? It's like a three-ring circus in here!"

"Great news, Jake," shouted Ricki, and she looked at him with a huge grin. "Cathy's back, freed from the bonds of fear, and she's going to ride Rashid again. Isn't that great? And Cheryl is getting Sheila, and we finally know who's responsible for this nasty business with our horses. Jake, it wasn't us! It was Sasha, who was jealous of Cheryl, and furious with everyone and everything! She poured perm solution over the halters!"

Jake looked at Ricki, incredulous, because he thought he had misunderstood, but when he saw that Carlotta was nodding her agreement, he seemed remorseful as he walked over to Ricki.

"I want to apologize to you and the others. I guess I was a little too hasty with my accusations. I'm very sorry," he said, and he left quickly.

Carlotta looked at Ricki, Lillian, and Kevin, who understood immediately what the look meant.

Ricki made her way over to Cathy and stretched out her

hands. "I have to apologize, too. I didn't mean to hurt your feelings, but I was so mad!"

Cathy wrapped her arms around her best friend. "Come here, you idiot! I was just as stupid. Let's just forget about it."

"Absolutely!" The two girls beamed at each other.

"And, Cheryl, we're sorry, too, that we suspected you."

"Oh, forget about it. It's been a bad day for all of us."

"But one that turned out well," added Cathy.

"Yes. If only our horses were well again, everything would be perfect," said Lillian, a little sadly.

"At least they'll be fine." Kevin decided to be upbeat. "We'll just ask the vet what we should put on those sores, and with luck they'll disappear like magic."

"Okay, that's exactly what we'll do. And we'll send the bill to Sasha, so she can be happy about the health of our animals, too," grinned Carlotta, who was glad that everything had been cleared up, and that she hadn't been wrong about Cheryl.

Affectionately, Carlotta gazed at one happy kid after the other, and then she tapped the floor with her crutch. "Okay, now I want to know which of the puppies you have left for me. When we get that cleared up, then I'll talk with your mother, Ricki, and have a cup of coffee before I leave to talk with Lillian's parents."

"Carlotta, you are just the best!" said Ricki, beaming, and hurried outside to call the puppies. "You get Lucky, and you won't pay us anything!" she called over her shoulder as she hurried away. "You're the kind of person who's always bringing others luck – so now, you'll have a little luck of your own!"